DOG DAYS FOR MARY BROWN

A NOVELLA

BERNICE BLOOM

Bernice Bloom

DEAR READERS

Hello,

Welcome to 'Dog Days' - the book in which Mary Brown throws caution to the wind and gets herself a puppy.

I know, I know... those of you who have read my previous books will be thinking that has disaster written all over it. Mary can barely look after herself. What is she thinking of getting an animal to look after?

You might also be thinking: why doesn't Ted stop her?

There's a very good reason for that: Ted has no idea that she's bought a puppy. Indeed, Ted has no idea until the puppy arrives at the door. Then it's too late.

But, hey - look on the bright side - maybe having a puppy will change Mary? She might become more organised and sophisticated as she is charmed by the new arrival. She might respond to her new responsibilities with alacrity. Perhaps she'll surprise us all...or perhaps not!

I really hope you enjoy it.

Lots of love, Bernice xx

NOTE: The puppy in the book is male, so the references to puppies are written in the masculine to reflect this. If you have a female puppy, I apologise, but the torturous process of writing he or she on every occasion was clumsy and difficult to sustain. This is a book about all puppies - male and female. They are all as mad, crazy and loveable as each other. Indeed, the maddest puppy I know is female (I'm looking at you, Molly Walker).

THE MARY BROWN BOOKS IN ORDER

IMPORTANT NOTE

This book was previously released as 'Adorable Fat Girl gets a Christmass puppy' but now has a new name and a sparkling new cover.

PROLOGUE

TWELVE THINGS YOU DON'T KNOW UNTIL YOU GET A PUPPY

1. The name you give your puppy is important. You will find yourself in many parks, shouting it very loudly while your puppy ignores you completely and everyone else listens in. If you're thinking of fanny, pussy, muff, pocket rocket, or rumple foreskin, DON'T DO IT!

2. You will read all the books about how to have a well-trained puppy who knows his place in the house, and you will break all the rules. He'll be in your bed, wearing your pyjamas and driving your car around by the end of the first week.

3. You'll be so delighted when he does a poo outside that you will clap your hands in joy and say something like, 'what a lovely big poo.' People will hear you, and they will judge you, and make sure they aren't the same people who saw you running through the park earlier shouting, 'rumple foreskin.'

4. Puppies follow you everywhere. I mean - everywhere. Fancy going to the loo by yourself?

Nope. Not happening. The bath? No. There'll be a little face peeking over the edge of the bath, watching your every move.

5. Puppies vomit more than you'd think they would. Then they eat it. Yep, you read that right. They eat their vomit. Can you imagine anything more disgusting in the whole of the universe? No? OK - try this - they also eat other dogs' poo. I KID YOU NOT!

6. Puppies and baths are a mad combination. Your puppy will go so insane afterwards that you'll think you've broken him. He'll race around the house as if he's in the Olympic 200m final...then up and over tables, jumping on everything and burying his head in things, stealing the towel you've carefully wrapped him in and casting it aside. Then, finally, he will race and skid in ever-decreasing circles. It's called the zoomies, and it's MAD. Puppies are MAD.

7. The peeing is unbelievable. You need to know the amount of pee a small puppy has inside of him. Loads! And he will want to wee on everything...marking his scent on every lamppost, postbox, street corner, every child who stands still for too long, inside people's handbags, over other dogs. The list is endless...as is the amount of urine that one tiny creature can create.

8. Humping. Oh yes. Are you having friends over for dinner? Then your dog will whip his genitals out in front of everyone and start licking them furiously, humping handbags and legs, oblivious as to how much embarrassment and consternation he's causing. You have to respect puppies. They can liven up any social gathering.

9. No one will ever see you pick up dog poo. But if you forget to bring a bag, you will find yourself surrounded by hundreds of people looking at you with judgement in their eyes, waiting for you to pick it up.
10. You can spend hundreds of pounds on expensive dog toys, but your dog's favourites will be toilet paper rolls, hair bands, and plant pots (that's my dog anyway - fill in your own odd collection of weird favoured items!).
11. Your dog will always do the cutest thing seconds after you put the camera away.
12. You will never believe how deeply you will fall in love with your furry friend.

CHAPTER 1

'What an incredible day,' says Ted, bursting through the door after whistling his way down the path to the house. 'The contract is signed. And it's all down to my negotiating skills. I'm on fire. Fancy going out for dinner tonight to celebrate?'

'That's incredible. Well done, angel,' I say.

I'm not entirely sure what Ted's job involves. He seems to spend a lot of time persuading people to sign contracts.

'So, dinner tonight?'

'Probably not tonight,' I say. 'Would be lovely to get a takeaway, though. It's so cold out there. On nights like these, I want to curl up on the sofa. Ideally, relaxing with a beautiful little puppy in the house would be lovely, don't you think?'

'Er...no. I'm going to shower. We should go out for dinner, though - we have something to celebrate.'

'I think I'd prefer to stay in.'

'OK. If you insist, let me know what takeaway you want.'

'A takeaway puppy, please.'

'Not going to happen,' he says as he strides towards the bathroom.

'Little puppy? Just a tiny one?'

'No.' He walks out of the sitting room, slamming the door behind him.

Now TED'S out of earshot; I need to tell you something. Don't judge me. Ted will do enough of that later. Just listen while I explain what I've done. But - beware - it's reckless and awful.

I bought a puppy without telling Ted anything about it.

I know, I know.

But hear me out - he's a beautiful little cavapoo with a button nose, eyes like melted chocolate, and a pale rust-coloured coat that makes him look exactly like a teddy bear. He's gorgeous. And I'm in love. So in love.

The slight problem is that the puppy is due to be delivered in half an hour and - as you heard - Ted is not keen. So I'm not sure what to do now.

I can hear the shower in the bathroom and Ted singing to himself as he washes. He's full of joy and optimism after a great day at work.

I suggested not going out to dinner tonight because I need to be in when the puppy arrives, and that's why I keep dropping hints the size of boulders about how much I'd like a puppy.

I know it's stupid of me, and I know you might be reading this and thinking that I'm a Goddamned idiot for not talking to my boyfriend before making such a huge life decision. I hear you! A Goddamned idiot is exactly what I am. But - my God - you should have seen that little puppy's pretty face. I've never seen anything so gorgeous in my whole life.

It all began four weeks ago when Charlie and Juan's next-door neighbour, Joy, declared that her dog, Flossie, had puppies. In case you're not fully up-to-date with all the goings-on in my life - Juan and Charlie are now flat-mates. Charlie moved out of her boyfriend Mike's apartment after discovering that he was an unfaithful louse, and she moved in with Juan.

The two of them kept talking about how lovely the puppies were. To start with, I was fairly nonplussed at the whole thing. Charlie was skipping around, telling me how pretty they were, how tiny, and how they were born on Christmas Eve, but I'm not a dog person. So I only went with her to see them because she kept on so much (and I hoped to bump into gorgeous Dave, who lives in the flat below Joy's).

So, off I went. I met up with Juan and Charlie, and we arrived at Joy's flat to find that she had put up this gate in the living room doorway to stop all the dogs from running around the house. We stood at it, waiting for Joy to let us in when a tiny puppy came skipping up to it and looked up at me with those heavenly eyes. I felt like I'd been hit by a truck. I swear I thought my heart was going to explode with love. I could feel my adoration for the little puppy squeezing my chest.

'This one's beautiful,' I said as calmly as possible, trying to make it sound like a casual observation, while deep inside, I was screaming with excitement and wanted to steal the puppy and run away. Joy opened the gate, and we went in. I sat on the sofa, and the same little angel came frolicking over to me and sat at my feet, looking up at me in a way that no one had ever looked at me before...a face full of trust, adoration, and curiosity. He dropped his little head to one side, and something in me gave an almighty twang.

'I want him,' I said in quite a scary voice.

'Blimey, are you OK?' asked Charlie.

Without taking my eyes off the puppy, I repeated myself.

'I want him.'

'But you need to check with Ted first,' she reasoned. 'He might not want a puppy.'

'I want him.'

I felt like a mother gazing into the eyes of her newborn baby boy and then being told that she might not be able to keep him.

I lifted the little puppy onto my lap, and he sat there, gently playing with the ridiculous Mickey Mouse motif on my t-shirt and chewing on my finger so gently that it felt as if he were brushing it with feathers.

'Listen, ladies, I have to go out now, but you're welcome to pop by any time,' said Joy.

'No,' I said, and Charlie looked at me sharply.

What's wrong with you? she mouthed.

'I love this puppy,' I said by way of explanation.

'The puppy's not ready to leave mum yet, but it will be in a couple of weeks,' said Joy. 'It's good that you love this little one; it's the only puppy that hasn't been bought yet.'

'It's not odd. It's destiny,' I said. Even Joy was looking a bit worried about me at this stage.

'Well, think about it and give me a ring when you decide. It's a big commitment, so don't rush into a decision.'

Charlie and I left, and it was as if I was in a trance for the rest of the day. It was as if I now knew what my life had been lacking all these years. A puppy. THAT puppy.

'You must check with Ted,' Charlie said over and over.

'I will,' I kept replying. And I meant to. Honestly, I did. But the time never seemed right. So, instead of talking it through with Ted, I contacted Joy and told her I wanted the puppy. I paid her a £500 deposit to secure the deal, and Joy said she would drop the puppy off today…in half an hour.

. . .

TED WALKS BACK in from the shower, whistling and smiling, still on a high after his corporate successes. He's dressed in his navy-blue towelling dressing gown. He looks lovely in it.

'Chinese?' he asks, dropping himself into the sofa and grimacing at the crunching sound it makes under his weight.

'Blimey - I need to get myself on a diet,' he says. 'But not tonight. Tonight, we will go mad. Tomorrow we will diet.'

I smile at him, but my insides are in turmoil.

'A feast for two?'

'Yes, let's get the royal feast for two,' I say because I know that's his favourite.

'And a little glass of wine?' he says.

'No, not tonight. I think I will have a night off the booze.'

Are you sure?' He sounds very surprised. I don't drink *that* much.

'Yes, I'll just have Diet Coke or something.'

I'm saying this because, in around 30 minutes, I will have a puppy to look after and an angry boyfriend to placate. I might even have to move out while he calms down. So the last thing I need is to be drunk.

'Are you ok?' asks Ted. 'You don't seem quite yourself.'

'I'm fine. Really. Just thinking about things.'

'Anything you want to talk about?'

Now I know this is the moment. This is the 'in' I've been waiting for. This is when I confess my sins, tell him every-thing, and apologise for being an idiot. But the words won't come. They're stuck in the back of my throat, unable to release themselves. Perhaps it's because I'm worried he'll make a tremendous fuss and tell me I can't have a puppy when I know that - even if he gave me an ultimatum and threatened to throw me out - I would still want the puppy. The passion with which I want this small dog is quite disturbing.

'It's coming in half an hour,' he says.

'You know! How do you know?'

'It says on Deliveroo. I threw in an extra curry and some chips, so there'll be plenty to eat.'

'Oh, the food will be here in half an hour. Oh, I see. Right, yes. Good.'

Ted glances at me as if I'm odd as he heads off to the kitchen to get out the plates. He pours a glass of wine while he's there, and wanders back into the sitting room to lay the small coffee table in front of us, so we can enjoy the Chinese while watching *Married at First Sight*.

There's a knock on the door while he's arranging the cutlery, and I feel myself stiffen. Ted jumps up and walks towards it, and it's like everything starts to move in slow motion.

'I hope you're hungry, Mary,' he says as he swings open the door.

I hear female voices, and Ted calls my name. I stand up slowly and walk out into the corridor where Joy and her daughter are standing, holding my beautiful puppy. My heart sings when I see his pretty face.

'I'm sorry, Ted. I'm really sorry,' I say. 'But I couldn't resist it…. I've bought a puppy.

CHAPTER 2

'OK, let me get this straight,' Ted is saying as he strides across the sitting room, biting into a spring roll and letting the flakes fall from his mouth onto the front of his dressing gown. 'You couldn't help yourself. You just had to get the puppy.'

'I'm sorry, Ted. I really am. And I kept wanting to tell you, but I was so scared.'

As I talk, tears run down my face. I'm cuddling the beautiful baby and am so full of love that I struggle to speak properly. I pull him closer, and he starts to lick my face.

'I'll do all the work...you don't need to do anything at all,' I say.

Ted slumps back down on the sofa and hears the enormous crunch sound again. 'For God's sake. Does the sofa need to do that? It's so judgemental,' he mutters.

'Look at him; he's licking away my tears,' I say.

Ted puts his head into his hands. 'Look - he's cute, and I can see how much you love him, but this is ridiculous. We're a partnership - you and I - you can't just run off and make a decision like that without consulting me. You know that I

11

don't want a pet, but you get one anyway. What sort of relationship is that?'

'I know,' I say. 'I know I was wrong, and I'm sorry. I don't know what to say.'

'And he's not sleeping in the bedroom. He sleeps in here.'

'Yes,' I say.

'We'll talk about this some more tomorrow, but the way I feel at the moment, I think you should take it back. It's just not right to do this to me.'

I feel the tears coming again, so I don't say anything.

'I'm going to bed.'

Ted stands up, and the sofa makes its wheezy crunchy sound again - he snarls at it and leaves the room without kissing me goodnight. He always kisses me goodnight. I'm left sitting there with a giant Chinese takeaway and a gorgeous puppy.

'Hello lovely,' I say to the little boy who has already brought so much chaos into my life. He licks my face. 'You're very lovely,' I say. 'I'm going to look after you and make you very happy.'

I play with my new puppy for a while and continue chatting with him when I hear Ted walking back down the stairs. He pops his head around the door frame, and I brace myself for more anger and condemnation.

'I've been listening to you talking to him,' he says. 'Like you're his mum or something.' His manner is very different now. He's speaking gently and looking at the puppy. 'Will you be OK with him, or do you need help?'

I have all the equipment, food, and other paraphernalia that I need, but I don't know what to do with it all. It would be great if he'd stay with me for a while.

'Will you help me?' I ask. 'I am sorry about this. Really, really sorry. I just fell in love with him straight away, and I couldn't help myself. I was stupid not to tell you, but I was terrified you'd say no. I don't know what else to say. I'm an idiot.'

'OK,' he says, looking at the puppy sitting there, looking back at him with those fabulous dark eyes. 'He is lovely. I can see why you fell for him. But you understand why I'm cross, don't you?'

I nod. Of course, I understand. He has every right to be cross.

'So, what do we need to do then?' he says, moving to perch himself on the edge of the sofa, then thinking better of it and moving away. The crunching sound it makes is getting to him. We both need to lose serious weight, but we don't need the sofa to remind us.

'We need to think of a name,' I say.

Ted shrugs, raising his shoulders to his ears and lifting the corner of his lip to meet his nose. 'I don't know,' he says.

'You look like Elvis Presley when you do that.'

He does it again, saying 'Blue Suede Shoes' in a southern drawl as he does so.

'Exactly like El… Oh, oh, oh…I've got it!' I say.

'Got what?'

'A name.'

'Go on then….'

'Elvis,' I say proudly. 'We should call him Elvis.'

I swear that, as I say this, the puppy looks up at me and drops his head to one side.

'He knows his new name,' says Ted, putting his arm around me and squeezing tightly. I burst into tears and lay my head on Ted's shoulder.

'I'm so happy,' I tell him. 'This is the greatest thing ever.'

Ted kisses me on the head. 'It's a top name,' he says. 'And we'll be able to talk in Elvis lyrics all the time. That'll be fun. It'll be worth calling him Elvis just for that.'

'Oh, definitely.'

'How does this all work now, then?' asks Ted. 'Where does he sleep? What does he eat? I don't know anything about puppies.'

'Everything I have bought for him is hidden upstairs in the linen cupboard,' I say.

'OK, do you want me to go and get it?'

'Yes, please. And - Ted - Thank you for not asking me to return to sender.'

'Don't worry; I'd never do that, Delilah.'

'Delilah?' I say as Ted stands up to go out to the linen cupboard where all my booty is hidden. 'Elvis Presley didn't sing Delilah, that was Tom Jones,'

'Elvis covered it as well,' he insists. 'My parents used to play an 'Elvis' Greatest Hits' album repeatedly. It was definitely on there.'

'Oh, right. I'd better do some Elvis Presley research.'

Elvis jumps into my lap as I say this and licks my face. I wonder whether I'll ever tire of him doing that. I know some people hate it when dogs lick their faces. Will I become like that? I can't ever imagine finding distaste in that lovely, affectionate gesture.

Ted's back a few minutes later with his arms full of boxes and bags. I expect him to start getting cross again because I've been planning this for a couple of weeks, but he doesn't get angry; he just lays it all down.

'What do I need to do?'

'He sleeps in this crate at night,' I say, indicating the large, brown box with a picture of a metal cage stuck onto it. 'But that looks like a jail,' he says. 'You didn't buy it so we could sing Jailhouse Rock, did you? Because if you did - I applaud you, but I also think it's a step so far. He can't sleep in that; it looks so unfriendly.'

'I know. I agree. That's what all the experts tell you to do, though. So I bought a soft bedding cushion that goes inside it and these drapes to go over it.'

'OK, let's get this setup then,' he says, tipping out the contents of the box. While he puts the crate together - clinking metal and securing latches, Elvis wanders around him - looking on, intrigued. I sit there and watch them both.

'I feel like I'm in a real family,' I say. 'I'm so happy.'

Ted leans over and kisses me.

'I know, sweetheart, he's really cute. I just wish we could have discussed this. It's such a big move.'

'I know. Thank you for helping.'

He smiles and returns to the crate.

I think I knew, deep down, that it would be alright with Ted in the end. I suspect I wouldn't have taken the risk and just gone off and got Elvis if I hadn't known that Ted would come around. I hadn't expected that he would be so helpful soon. I thought he'd sulk for a couple of days before relenting.

I look down at Elvis - he's every bit as beautiful as I remember him being, with his floppy ears and fur an enviable russet-blonde colour. I might take him with me when I next go to the hairdresser and get mine done in exactly the shade. Would that be odd? Would the hairdressers all think I'd lost my marbles? Yes, probably. No, I won't do that. I'll take a picture instead.

'OK, all fixed up,' says Ted, sitting back on his heels and looking proudly at the metal cage in front of him.

'Thank you,' I say. 'Life is wonderful. I can't imagine anything going wrong.'

'Well, let's hope not. Are you going to put him in there now? It's getting quite late.'

'Yes, I'll put the covers over it first and make it as un-jail-like as possible, then I'll be up. This is going to be fantastic.'

.   .   .

1 AM:

The house is cold, and my bed is warm. There's a sound coming from the sitting room.

OH, my God. What is wrong now? Elvis is crying again. I don't know what to do. I put him into his crate at 10.30 pm; then I came back down when he cried at midnight and settled him. I stroked him and spoke to him and calmed him down. I thought he might sleep through until morning, but now he's crying again. Of course, Ted is managing to sleep through the whole thing. The only thing louder than the crying downstairs is the sound of Ted's snoring upstairs.

I slip on my dressing gown and head back down, not knowing whether I'm doing the right thing. I've read a lot of books that say you shouldn't take the puppy out of the crate, or they will learn that crying means they get to leave the crate, which will prompt them to cry much more. You can, however, go down and check that they are OK and comfort them through the bars. So that's what I'm doing. Perhaps I shouldn't. Who knows? But it's the little puppy's first night here, and he's terrified... So I have to soothe him.

I stroke him through the bars, but he pushes himself up against the metal as if he wants to reach me, so eventually, I surrender and open the crate. He bounds into my arms, and I cuddle him while he calms down and eventually falls asleep.

I lay him back in his crate.

As soon as he's in there, I stand up to move away but the minute I get to my feet and step towards the door, he cries. I don't know what to do. I don't want him to cry. I don't want him to be sad. Not ever. So I go back to the crate and start stroking him again.

I decide the next time I stop stroking him and move away; I'll ignore the crying and keep moving. But it's no good at all. He cries louder. I might be here for the rest of my life - stroking, moving away, stroking again, moving away.

In the end, I pull the crate towards the sofa and lie down while still stroking him. Then, finally, he falls asleep.

AT 3 AM, I wake with a jolt. Where the hell am I? I turn to the right and see bars. Oh My God - I'm in jail. What did I do? Why am I locked away? Then I hear an animal cry from the crate next to my head. I'm in a zoo. What the hell sort of night did I have that ended up with me falling asleep in a zoo?

Then it comes flooding back. I have a puppy. He's called Elvis. He's a lovely puppy, and I adore him, but he doesn't like sleeping all that much.

There's another cry from the crate. Not a gently muffled sound that one might expect a tiny, sweet puppy to make, but more an all-out growl for attention. I move my head to sit up. My neck is sore after sleeping on the sofa with it all scrunched up. I can turn it to the right, but it feels like my whole neck is seizing up when I move it to the left. It's also really cold. I should have got a spare duvet and put it over me on the sofa. I hope Elvis is warm enough. Perhaps that's why he's crying?

I open the gate to the crate, and he bounds out and up to me, furiously licking my face as if I've just returned from eight years at war. I lift him into my arms and bring him onto the sofa next to me, cuddling him gently as he falls asleep in my arms.

And that's where we stay, with him having managed to get himself out of the crate on the first night. This, ladies and gentlemen is known as 'building a rod for your own back.' I know this because every book and every website tells me so.

'Above all, do not take the puppy out of the crate,' they all say with determination. 'You must leave the puppy in the crate and train him to stay in there. If you take him out, getting him back in there the next night will be very hard.'

WHEN I HEAR the heavy thud of Ted's footsteps coming downstairs, I stand up and position myself near the front of the cage as if I've just taken him out.

'You're up early,' he says.

'Yes, I thought I'd come and see him,' I say. 'Isn't he a good boy?'

'He is,' says Ted. 'He slept all through the night without crying - he's a very good boy. But what are you going to do about work today?'

'I'm off this week to look after him, then Charlie said she would help because she's working from home now, and Juan said he's happy to pop over if we need him.'

'Oh good. OK. And you've remembered I'm not home tonight, haven't you? I'm in Manchester for the northern sales dinner.'

'Right,' I say. 'OK, that's no problem.'

In truth, it is a bit of a problem; I'd much prefer Ted to be around. It's scary having a little, tiny animal's life in your hands. I thought that having a little puppy would be like having a teddy bear, but it's quite frightening. They are so little and vulnerable.

'I'm going to have a shower and pack some things. You two behave yourselves, won't you?'

'Of course.' I say.

'And don't get any more bloody pets while I'm away.'

'I'll try not to.'

· · ·

THE NEXT NIGHT, while Ted's away, I go to bed with Elvis in my arms. I walk upstairs, cuddling him to my chest before laying him in the bed. Elvis looks at me, thrilled by this unlikely turn of events. He doesn't know what to do, so he runs around, jumping on the duvet and making happy noises. The sounds he's making are very different from the squealing noises of sadness that emanated from that crate last night. That's it. He's sleeping with me. Ted will be about as unimpressed as a man can be, but, as always, he'll forgive me. I know he will.

The next day, Ted comes back, and he does forgive me.

Two days after that, we fold the crate up and slip it under the sofa, where we forget about it for two years until we move house.

CHAPTER 3

'*H*appy Birthday to you, Happy birthday to you. Happy Birthday dear Elvis. Happy Birthday to you.'

'Are you going to sing that every week for the next 10 or so years?' asks Ted, as I cuddle Elvis close to me, and kiss him on the top of his head.

'Yep.'

'You don't think that we should save the singing for the traditional birthday celebrations? They come once a year.'

'Nope. He's 13 weeks old today and look how perfect he is. We should celebrate that every week.'

'Mad,' says Ted, stepping out of bed and striding through to the bathroom. 'That puppy has driven you to even greater heights of madness than you reached before. And - let's be fair, Mary, you were already quite mad.'

In many ways it feels like five minutes since there was a knock on the door and a look of surprise on Ted's face as a puppy arrived in his home; in other ways, it feels like I've had Elvis all my life. He's so much part of the family and such a huge part of my world now that I can't remember what life was like before he came along.

It's not all glorious and wonderful, of course, I'm struggling with the toilet training and the biting. Then there's the crying noise he makes when I leave him alone for more than a second. It cuts right through me.

Now our journey is set to take a step in a new direction as he goes for his final vaccinations at the vet's today. It means that in a few days' time, I'll be able to take him outside...go for walks and sit in cafes while he curls up by my feet. I'll be able to have a life with him that is not within these four walls.

'Come on then,' says Ted. 'Let's get this little man jabbed.'

'We have an appointment at 10 am,' I tell the receptionist.

'Oh, let me see him,' she says, walking out and stroking Elvis. 'What a lovely little thing. What's his name?'

'Elvis.'

'Oh, great name. Take a seat and the vet will be with you shortly.'

Ted sits down while I look around. There are posters on the walls of the surgery from people offering all sorts of services: dog walking, puppy training, and problem-solving. I pull out my phone to take a picture of the puppy training poster, then read down through the other notes.

Someone is selling a crate 'lightly used' and I think of our crate, languishing beneath the sofa. I'm not sure that ours would even qualify as 'lightly used' to be honest. We gave up on all that pretty promptly.

There are people offering bereavement counselling for those whose pets have died. Christ, that's a terrifying thought. I move my eyes quickly away from the sad page and to two large posters at the bottom. That's when my heart really stops.

'Important information,' reads the first one. 'Dognappers

are operating in this area. Make sure you follow these rules...'

It then goes on to advise making sure that you don't let your dog off the lead anywhere near car parks where someone could grab your puppy and throw them into a car. *Use common sense, leave the area if you see anyone suspicious-looking, and always be alert.* Bloody hell.

The second poster is even more graphic, it tells of a specific incident in Bushy Park, one of the big royal parks near us where I had envisaged myself leaping and dancing around with Elvis. 'Ted, come and see this,' I say, beckoning him, and instructing him to look at the poster.

'Yes, I saw something about that on the news yesterday, it's getting more and more common. I guess the price of puppies has gone up so much during lockdown that it's like stealing an expensive watch,' he says.

'What?? It's nothing like stealing an expensive watch. Elvis is my flesh and blood.'

'Well, no - he's not, is he? I know you love him, and no one's going to steal him from you, but you didn't give birth to him.'

'Well, I love him as much as if I had.'

'OK, I was just trying to explain why it's so common for dog napping to take place these days.'

'So common? You make it sound like puppies are being stolen every day. Nobody can steal my puppy. If they steal my puppy, I'll kill them. I'd die if he went missing.'

'He won't,' says Ted with certainty.

BUT HE'S WRONG.

We don't know it as we stand there in the safety and warmth of the surgery, but Elvis will go missing, and - yes - I do almost die from the pain of it all.

.   .   .

THE VET COMES out to talk to us. She strokes Elvis and gives him a quick once-over. She's a kindly-looking Chinese woman in a white coat and rather smart spectacles. She starts to explain about the vaccinations, but I've only got one thing on my mind. 'That all sounds fine. But is it possible to get a harness and lead with an alarm on? I'm worried about him being stolen.'

'I don't think so. You can get leads with trackers on that link to your phone, so you can find your puppy if he runs off, but I don't think they're alarmed.'

'Can you get them made so that they deliver an electric shock to anyone who touches the lead except for Ted and me?'

'No, that's not possible.'

'Someone should invent one. How about ones with a forcefield around the puppy so no one can get close.'

The vet glances at me, half-smiles, and returns to looking at Elvis. 'The puppy looks lovely and healthy. Let's take him to be weighed; then we can administer the injection.'

The vet does a full check of Elvis, then declares, 'He's a little on the skinny side.'

'Same as me!' I say.

'Yeah, it's always been a problem in our house,' adds Ted.

The vet looks up at us. We weigh about 40 stones between us. She smiles and returns to examining Elvis without comment.

'He's a very healthy little man. Just make sure he's eating enough. When he starts going out and exercising, he'll use a lot of energy, so it's important to make sure he's well-fed. Let's get this vaccination done.'

She takes Elvis into a back room while Ted and I wait. We hear a rather loud howl; we are presented with a rather

23

large bill, and soon we're back in the car and heading home.

'Can we stop at the pet store and get some more food and some treats on the way back?' I ask Ted. 'I don't like the idea of him being too skinny.'

CHAPTER 4

So, today's been an interesting day. I've had Elvis for three months, but I discovered, for the first time, that Elvis doesn't like brushes. When I say he doesn't like them, I mean he can't abide them…. he doesn't want them in the house. He hates floor brushes, nail brushes, Ted's shaving brush - all of them.

But he reserves particular disdain for hairbrushes.

When I'm brushing my hair, he goes nuts… he barks like a lunatic and swings his paw up as if to try and grab it from me. It is so disturbing that I often abandon all efforts to tame my hair with a brush and resort to fingers.

I got halfway through brushing my hair this morning and couldn't stand the whining and barking anymore, so I let him have the brush. He's same if I try to brush him. It's fine when I run my hands through his fur. Indeed, it's fine if I run anything else over him, but as soon as it's a brush, he barks and barks and snatches it off me. If I don't let him have the brush, he makes a menace of himself and tries to grab other things.

He was behaving in a particularly grabby way this morning, so I got dressed in a bit of a hurry, trying to stop him from grabbing my bra out of my hands as I put it on. This involved me running around the bedroom as he followed behind, trying to get hold of the bra by its straps, then trying to bite my knickers as I slipped into them. I felt like I was in some terrible Benny Hill sketch.

Then I made the mistake of putting on a maxi dress. He saw that as a sign of great fun to come as he leapt and jumped and tried to grab the back of the dress. I walked out of my bedroom with him attached by his teeth and claws.

'Elvis, let go.' I tried in my firmest voice. He was sitting on the back of the dress, pulling it down, his mouth firmly attached. There was a great deal of me spinning around, trying to get him to release his teeth before I knelt down and unhooked his claws from the hem of the flouncy dress, and stood up. It didn't work. He immediately jumped back onto the dress and grabbed it in his mouth again.

Good lord. Whose idea was it to get a puppy? This was getting ridiculous.

There was only one thing for it - I needed to lift the dress away from his gaze, so I hoiked up the back of it and stuff it into my knickers so he couldn't get it.

With the temptation of the dress out of sight, he immediately relaxed and followed me as I went into the bathroom, did my makeup as quickly as possible, and headed downstairs.

I knew that a long walk would tire him out and give me a bit of peace, so I put on his harness and lead and walked out of the door.

Now there is definitely something about having a dog that makes you forgetful. I know people who have babies talk about doing all sorts of silly things in the early days because of the hormones coursing around the body. I know that having a puppy isn't quite the same as that; I didn't give birth to him or anything, as Ted reminds me, but I definitely feel a bit useless and forgetful. I guess you're so distracted by making sure the puppy is okay, not damaging anything, and not damaging themselves, that you forget to think about yourself.

So I am oblivious as I walk along and smile warmly at the man next door. 'How are you getting on with Elvis?' he asks.

'Oh, absolutely fine.'

'I hear him barking. I wondered whether everything was okay.'

'All fine. He barks sometimes because he's young and he doesn't understand, but he's OK. He doesn't disturb you, does he?'

'Not at all,' he says as he heads back inside, no doubt to complain to his wife about how much Elvis is disturbing them. I walk onto Bridge Road and stride down past the Lebanese restaurant in the direction of the river. I haven't gone far when I hear a voice coming from behind. It's my neighbour, running along behind me.

'Say, Mary, I'm sorry to interrupt you, but did you mean to have your dress stuffed in the back of your knickers?'

'Good God, no,' I exclaim, unravelling the maxi dress from its place in my underwear where I had stuffed it earlier to stop Elvis from jumping up and down on it. 'Thank you for letting me know.'

The man next door (I must find out what his name is, I can't keep calling him that) gives a sort of snort and turns back to go into his house. I feel a wave of embarrassment come crashing down on me. Poor man...he's just had full sight of my enormous knickers. No one deserves that.

I continue walking down towards the river, glancing at the beautiful little shops as I go past. There's a lovely clothes shop with the most beautiful jewellery and these elegant dresses that I will definitely come and buy when I've lost weight (just around the time that hell freezes over). I glance in the window at a rather beautiful khaki jacket with this brightly coloured braiding on it. As I look, I spot my reflection looking back at me. Oh God, could today get any worse? One side of my hair is neatly brushed and hanging elegantly over my shoulders. The other half is all scrunched up and in a terrible mess. It looks as if I forgot to brush half of it.

Then I remember...that moment in the bedroom when I'd been forced to hand over the brush to an angry Elvis. I *have* only brushed half of it.

Oh lord. I'm a laughing stock.

No one tells you this stuff before you get a puppy.

CHAPTER 5

I walk the rest of the distance to the park next to the river while frantically smoothing down my hair. At least when I'm off the High Street, fewer people will see me.

The entrance to Hurst Park is next to the cricket club and the rather lovely boat club, full of beautiful men in lycra, and young women with swishy ponytails.

I see three rather elegantly dressed blonde women, all with small dogs like mine, waiting by the entrance to the cricket club as we walk past. I've seen them before, from a distance, never close enough to talk to, or smile at, or anything. They are not the sort of women who would usually pay me any attention at all. They look amazing, slim, and well-dressed. I, on the other hand, look like nothing so much as an overweight bag lady, and I'm not really being fair to bag ladies when I say that. Groups of beautiful women like that don't tend to acknowledge me. I'm not putting myself down - just stating a simple fact: the beautiful people are from another planet, they do things differently from the rest of us, and they keep to themselves.

But, to my amazement, they acknowledge me today.

They all sigh and clutch their chests when they see Elvis. They comment on how lovely he is and bend down to stroke him. He takes himself up onto his hind legs and licks their faces affectionately, nuzzling against them.

'Oh my God,' they squeal. 'He's beautiful.'

'Thank you,' I say as if it's got anything at all to do with me.

Then we leave and walk into the park. And I feel great. When you're overweight, you can feel ignored & overlooked, and you always feel judged, but since I've had Elvis, I haven't felt that. It's as if puppies provide a bridge between the thin and fat people, the ugly and the beautiful, rich and poor.

We all love puppies; they unite us.

Once we're in the park, I watch as Elvis runs up to every dog he sees, sniffing every bottom in the vicinity as he wags his tail with pure joy.

There are people in the park who I've got to know over the past few weeks; one is a little dog called Walnut. He is a bit of a pest, to be honest, but his owner is lovely. He's what we dog people call a 'ball thief'. Anyone who throws a ball anywhere near him will have it stolen. It doesn't matter that he's already got a ball of his own and doesn't need another; the little terror loves the attention he gets.

Walnut and his owner are here today, and I know exactly what will happen. I throw the ball, and Walnut comes bounding over, running like lightning towards the ball. Elvis gets there first and is about to pick the ball up when Walnut runs up to him, steals it, and is galloping off towards the children's playground; tail held high, delight emanating from every pore.

Walnut's delight is Elvis's dismay. My puppy looks at me appealingly as if to say, 'don't just stand there; get it back for me.'

So, I try. Walnut's owner tries too. Then another man joins in.

The three of us go running after Walnut, clutching packets of dog biscuits in the hope that he will drop the ball to take a treat from us. It's quite a circus as we jog along behind him, calling his name.

Eventually, the treats prove too much of a distraction for the little dog, and he drops the ball. Elvis piles in and grabs it back, and the two of us carry on our merry way.

The next stop on our journey is the bench in the centre of the park, situated next to a cluster of trees. I have to stop and take in the beauty of this pretty park by the river from time to time. I didn't even know the park existed before Elvis came along, and now it's like a second home.

Honestly, the park feels so familiar to me; I saw it in winter when my puppy first came along, carrying him in a sling when he was too young to walk, and then I brought him for his first stroll here in March. Now the place is warming up as spring approaches, and it looks so different. There's a lighter feel to the place. The snap and cold have been replaced by a gentle warmth; leaves are appearing on trees, and the sunlight catches the river, making it shine as if it's been polished. The boats that sit along the river feel alive with activity…people sit out next to them on colourful deckchairs, no longer locked away inside them. And there are so many more people in the park than there were in winter. It was beautiful, eerie, and mystical when covered in frost in February, but now it's as if life has been breathed into every part of it.

Sitting on the end of the bench is a man I've seen on every occasion that I've been in this park. I've nicknamed him Shaky because he always misquotes Shakespeare whenever I see him.

Today he has a book open in his lap, as he always does,

and his long, aged fingers slowly turn the pages. But he's not looking at the words on the page; he's looking out for people who will come over and talk to him about the book that he's not really reading.

His old dog sits patiently by his feet. Man, and dog, both waiting for company.

Elvis spots Shaky and runs over to him. He's had lots of treats from this lovely man in the past, so he knows there's a chance of some chicken if he plays his cards right. He stops abruptly in front of the man, wagging his tail furiously. Shaky strokes him. Then Elvis turns his attention to Shaky's dog - a rather scruffy little thing. I have no idea how old the dog is, but the speed with which he raises himself onto his legs indicates that he's seen around 300 summers.

Shaky lifts his arm and offers a gentle wave to me as Elvis cavorts on the grass in front of him, running around the older dog, backing away, jumping on top of him and trying to encourage him to play.

'You look well today, Lady Mary,' says Shaky in his mellifluous, Scottish-accented voice. I'm embarrassed that he knows my name because I don't have a clue what his name is. That's why I've nicknamed him 'Shaky'. He must have told me, but I simply don't remember. I know that his dog is called Burns, after Robert Burns, the Scottish poet. I know the names of most of the dogs in the park but none of the names of the owners.

'You're looking well too, sir,' I reply, taking a seat next to him.

'You're too kind,' he says. 'Much too kind.'

Shaky lays his book down on the bench next to him, lifts his head, and begins his traditional misquoting of Shakespeare. I love this part of my trips to the park. I mean, I don't know much about Shakespeare. I studied his plays at school like everyone else, but I wouldn't know whether his words were accurate or not. However, Shaky misquotes them with such wild abandon that you'd have to be insane not to realise he'd got them wrong.

'Out of my way you spot,' he says. 'You are a spot I don't want.'

'Very good,' I say, of his butchering of Macbeth. 'Really good.'

I've got a present with me for Shaky. It's something I saw in a second-hand shop and couldn't resist it.

'I come bearing a gift, ' I say, handing him the neatly wrapped parcel tucked away in my dog bag. He looks utterly delighted, with wide eyes and a wide smile, as he gently takes the paper off the book. The book is called 'Shakespeare's Best Lines.' He smiles at me as he opens the cover and reads the little tribute I've penned inside.

'To the man who makes me smile as much as a pint of beer by quoting all the great lines from a man known as Shakespeare.'

OK, OK, I know I'm not going to win any poetry awards, but I thought I'd write something, and that was the best I could do.

Shaky reaches out and touches my arm. His eyes are full of tears. 'I don't know when anyone last gave me a gift,' he said. you're a good friend to me, Lady Mary, and so is Elvis. You're a kind person.'

'I hope you enjoy it,' I say. I didn't realise this would all be so emotional. Then he sits and looks at me with such love and adoration that I think I'm going to start crying too.

'I will enjoy this," he says. 'I'll enjoy it so much. I haven't read any Shakespeare properly for years. I sometimes think I'm getting the words wrong when I sit here talking to people. I'll be able to check now, won't I.'

He says this with a wink, and I wonder whether he knows he's misquoting.

'But I like the words the way you say them,' I say, realising how much I love to hear him getting the word of the most famous writer in the English language all jumbled up.

I sit down next to him while the dogs play in front of us, and he seems lighter, younger, and much happier than I've seen him look before. He usually looks sad, as if he's carrying around great pain with him. Now it seems as if his mood is lifted just a little. And all for £1.99. I definitely should buy more people little gifts for no reason. Why wait for Christmas and birthdays if you can make people smile like that on a random morning in May?

CHAPTER 6

'*I*'m looking forward to today,' I say to Ted as he pulls really weird faces into the mirror. First, his top lip is dragged right down over his teeth, and he's staring like a lunatic as he shaves. Then he pulls over the right side of his face to shave the left side before dropping his head back and jutting out his chin to reach underneath where his chin reaches his neck. It's quite a performance, like an elaborate mating dance from some rare and colourful bird.

'What's happening today then? What are you looking forward to?'

'I've got the puppy training session. Do you remember? It's a three-hour introduction to puppy training to see whether I want to sign up for the course.'

'Oh yes. Should be good.'

He's gone back to facial gymnastics, so I continue.

'Yeah, I guess. Of course, Elvis is well-behaved, so there shouldn't be any real issues, and we're not having problems, are we?'

'He's a good little boy, but it would be useful to pick up

some tips - especially for walking him off the lead near a road. We should be able to do that soon.'

'Should we? He's still young. Only six months. What if he runs into the road or runs away from us? Remember all those posters we saw in the vets? I still have nightmares about those.'

Puppy training classes are being held in a field around five miles away. Elvis and I are the first to arrive on this lovely June day, so we head up to where a circle of chairs is laid out next to a box of dog toys and water bowls.

It's not long before others have joined us - a range of anxious-looking people walk across the field with dogs of various shapes and sizes.

When we introduce ourselves, we do so by our dog names. I don't know the name of the large man in the khaki jacket; I only know that his little grey puppy is called shadow.

The lady in charge of transforming us from a rag-tag jumble of useless dog owners into efficient and commanding leaders of our pets is called Carmen. She has a mop of bright blonde hair that's so chaotic it looks like she has it on back-ward and bright blue eyes framed by blue eyeshadow and fringed by long eyelashes.

She explains that she lives in a caravan on the site, so she is there day and night. That immediately makes me think of her as an elaborate gypsy and wonder what on earth led her to live in a rather remote field.

'I know everything about dogs and will help us overcome any problems you're having. And my knowledge is special because everything I know, I learned from dogs,' she says.

For me, this is the most joyful news imaginable. Carmen is a little bit bonkers. That's ideal. Everyone should be a little bit bonkers. But big Terry at the back is less impressed.

'You learned from dogs?' he challenges.

'I did,' she says sharply. 'All my learning has come through the dogs themselves...through listening to them and watching them. Understanding them. They are the perfect teachers.'

'So you haven't got, like, a diploma in animal psychology or anything like that?'

'I have a PhD, actually,' she says.

'Oh, what in?' asks the owner of Shadow.

'In dogs. Just in dogs. OK? Happy now. Right, let's get going.'

I strongly suspect that this lady from the caravan does not have any PhD, let alone one in 'dogs.' Not that that bothers me in the least. I want a few tips to help me to train Elvis properly, and I'm keen for Elvis to meet other dogs. That's all I want. Quite what Big Terry at the back is hoping to get from today is entirely his business.

WE BEGIN the session by dividing ourselves into two groups: big dogs and small dogs. This is a relief. There are some quite beastly animals in the class, and I don't like the idea of Elvis having to deal with them. He's got such incredibly little legs. Have you ever noticed that? Dogs have very thin legs for the size of their body. I worry about things like this way more than I should.

We begin by walking the dogs around, letting them meet one another, sniff one another, and get used to being in the company of lots of other puppies. Elvis is quite happy - sniffing bottoms and licking other dogs' testicles before sniffing their faces. There are a couple of dogs - one called Candy Floss and one called Barry - who he doesn't take to at all, but he's happy with the others and even developing a little skip as he goes from one dog to the next.

Carmen urges us to talk to the other group members, share problems and discuss the issues we face.

I team up with Shadow's owner for a chat in the morning sunshine. He seems to have had more than his fair share of problems...the innocent-looking puppy in front of us has eaten a curry left out on the side and been so ill with diarrhoea that the family had to move out of the flat for the day and get professional cleaners in.

'That's not as bad as Muffin,' says a slim lady dressed in a Barbour jacket and wellies, as if she's off on a hunt. 'Muff is very lazy. She climbs onto the coffee table and jumps through the window to save her from walking around and through the door. She does it every time, but last night it was chilly, so we closed the window. We heard this big thump and went into the sitting room to see her splayed across the table. If it had been a cartoon, she'd have those stars spinning around her head.'

I can't compete with all this, but I join in by telling them about my embarrassing dress in the knickers moment and not being able to brush my hair.

'Ah, that's why your hair is in such a mess this morning,' says the Barbour lady.

'Actually - no - I managed to brush my hair this morning,' I respond.

Cheeky woman.

THAT NIGHT I have the most vivid dream. It's all about the precious thinness of dogs' legs. I told you I worry about things like this, and now the worry has seeped from daytime to nighttime. There's just no escaping my overactive imagination. In my dream, I decide to act upon my fears that a dog's skinny little legs aren't fit for purpose. They're not strong enough to cope with all the running, jumping, and bounding through the park that they do. They might break, and that would be beyond awful.

So, in my sophisticated design studio in central London that I share with Kate Moss and Pablo Picasso (I wish you could take things out of dreams and slot them into ordinary life), I design a wonderful suit of armour to sit over a puppy's legs to keep them safe when they are out and about in the park. The suit of armour is an incredible feat of engineering, featuring the most durable yet pliable, lightweight metals in the world. Great engineers are marvelling at my work, and I have become world-famous.

The armour construction is very effective because it's two layers thick (as I explain to Holly Willoughby on *This Morning*). 'You see, Holly, the metal needed to be able to bend and would need joints.'

Holly nodded as I spoke, and then Prince Charles appeared on a video link into the studio to commend me on my work. I think that Barack Obama was there, too; I remember him patting me on the back while Kate Moss and Picasso cheered.

When I wake up in the morning, I am genuinely disappointed that I haven't invented a suit of armour for dogs.

'What's the matter?' asks Ted when I stomp out of bed.

'Nothing. Nothing at all. I'm perfectly fine. A few hours ago, I had a magnificent design studio in central London and was praised by Holly Willoughby and Prince Charles. I'd invented a suit of armour to keep all puppies safe. But not now. No Kate Moss, no Pablo Picasso. Life is shit.'

'Perhaps you need a day off,' he says. 'You're talking absolute nonsense.'

CHAPTER 7

*I*t's only been seven months since Elvis came skipping into my life, but everything has changed beyond recognition since he arrived. It's the mornings that have transformed themselves the most. These days it's not an alarm clock that wakes me up. Instead, I'm pushed out of bed by a furry little creature who taps me on my shoulder and then nudges me with his paw until I sit up. If I ignore him, he'll lick my face like crazy until it's soaking wet, then start barking at me and jumping all over me. There's no escape.

We've got our ritual down to a T now. Once he's got me fully awake, at around 6 am, I walk into the kitchen, put the kettle on, and then open the doors into the garden. This is one of the loveliest things about the arrival of summer; we open the doors in the morning, and they stay open for most of the day so that Elvis can run in and out at will. It's September now, and we've cracked the toilet training, thanks to the fact that Elvis can get outside whenever he needs to. I'm not much looking forward to winter in a few months and having to close the doors to keep out the cold.

One of the other delights of the morning is the search for squirrels...every morning, as soon as the doors open, Elvis races out and stands on the small decking area to get the best possible view of the fence where the squirrels often gather. Should he see a squirrel trotting along the fence, or on a branch or the rooftops of the neighbouring buildings, he goes absolutely nuts, barking and jumping up and down, running in circles and generally acting with all the delight and sophistication of a drunk man who's been told he can have another pint.

Elvis tries to reach the squirrels, but given his inability to run up trees and walk along thin fences, he's no match for them. The squirrels scrabble away from him every time, and he's left standing there barking after their furry tales.

After the excitement of the squirrel chase, I put some food out for Elvis while I drink my coffee. That's when the badgering begins. Elvis is desperate to go out to the park from the moment he opens his little eyes, and once he sees me drinking coffee, it's like he knows it's almost playing time.

He wants to go to the park because he has developed this obsession with the ball. And when I say 'obsession,' I don't say it lightly. He is completely in love with anything that can be thrown and retrieved by him. This is usually a ball, of course, but on one of our early walks, I threw the ball a little too hard, and it landed in the river. Elvis didn't seem to understand that this meant there was no ball now, and he continued to bark at me and stand on his back legs, walking alongside me like a meerkat in the hope that he might persuade me to produce the ball from somewhere.

So frustrated was I, on this occasion, that I quickly finished drinking the coffee I was holding and scrunched up the cup, throwing it so that Elvis could retrieve it. We went through the park like this, with me hurling the coffee cup and Elvis picking it up until we reached the gates to the main road.

The park has been great over the summer. All those characters who seemed like dots on the landscape of our walk in the early days are now intricate parts of our daily life, asking after Elvis, offering him treats, and brightening the morning with small talk and warm greetings.

This morning I head out as usual, with Elvis freaking out with joy when I say the word 'walk' – honestly, he goes nuts when he hears the word. It's like I've given him drugs...he races around, jumps up, and becomes quite beside himself with joy.

In common with so many dog owners, we can't ever use the word 'walk' unless it directly relates to taking him for a walk. We have to spell it out in normal conversation so he doesn't lose his mind at the thought of it. We also have to spell out b-a-l-l rather than say the word. I'll tell you what - if dog ownership does nothing else for you, it teaches you to spell.

He will soon learn what the spellings mean. Then we'll be forced to think of something else. Perhaps we'll communicate in Russian or something; then, when he understands Russian, we'll have to start spelling things out in Russian. It's hard to imagine where this will all end. I'll be fluent in a range of odd languages - from Ancient Greek to Latvian - by the time he's a year old.

I'm MEETING my friend Juan at the end of the road for the walk today. He's not shown much interest in Elvis in all the time I've had him. He's not a dog-walking person - he's more catwalk than dog walk. But he's met a new man who loves dogs, and Juan is trying to learn about the beauty of dog ownership to impress him.

'Come on then,' I say to Elvis as we wander out of the front door and down the road towards the park. He sniffs gate posts and lampposts as we pass through the front door. He's started lifting his leg when he pees now. He lifts it so high into the air that I think he's going to fall over. But he has considerable balance for such a chaotic little puppy and is almost balletic as he brings it back down from its high arabesque and continues trotting along.

We walk past the cafes dotted along the end of the road, and I pull him to the other side of me. I learned my lesson a few weeks ago when he was cafe-side instead of roadside. He tried to mount a terrier, started licking this rather smart lady's barefoot inside her open-toe shoe, and then peed all over her skirt. Honestly, his manners are utterly appalling.

I'm aware that the question of whether I should get him 'done' is now hovering over me…I've read all about it, and I know it will stop him 'spraying' everywhere, will reduce the amount he barks, and will lead to him having a longer, healthier life, but - honestly, the thought of cutting this beautiful creature's balls off fills me with fear and dread. Ted thinks I'd be mad to do it, but the vet says it will help him be healthier. Christ, the decisions you must make when you're a dog owner.

Juan is standing at the end of the road, and I can see him from about a mile away. He's wearing his favourite sparkly leggings in midnight blue, a thin-looking V-neck sweater on top and a pink beret on his head; he has the most extraordinary little pink shoes on his feet. Over his arm lays a pale blue fur gilet.

On the other hand, I am wearing tracksuit bottoms tucked into big walking boots. On top, I am wearing a man's shirt and a gilet with lots of pockets that are stuffed full of dog treats, a water bottle, a ball, and my phone.

It's not cold, but the leaves are beginning to fall, so the

ground, while a beautiful carpet of gold and orange leaves, is also a bit mushy and slippy. So his little pink shoes aren't ideal for the task before us.

'Are you going to be OK like that?' I ask him. 'It can be a bit muddy and slippy in the park.'

'Am I going to be OK like this? Surely the question should be - aren't you going to be arrested for crimes against fashion like that?' he responds.

'But it's a dog walk, not a fashion show,' I try, but I'm quite envious...I have adopted the look of a middle-aged bird watcher for walks, and he looks so cool, glamorous, and fashionable ALL THE TIME. It looks like he's taking me out for the day as part of his community service work.

'Come on,' he says. 'Let's go and walk this little bundle of gorgeousness. You need to tell me about dogs so I can impress Ripple.'

'Ripple. That's a sweet name. How old is he, and what breed?'

Juan looks confused. 'He's 36, and he's Italian.'

'Oh, I thought Ripple was the dog's name.'

'Nope. Ripple's the very handsome man's name. No idea about the dog.'

'Well then, your first lesson in appealing to a dog owner is - always ask about the dog. I know the dogs' names in the park without knowing very many of the people's names.'

We reach the park, and Elvis starts pulling, eager to go and explore. I make him sit before loosening the lead, then I take the lead away, and he bounds across the grass, running in a big loop. He doesn't go far...this is the thing with cavapoos - they are real home birds. It's great when you're out in the park, it means they come back when you call them, and they rarely move far from your side. It's less fun when you're at home wanting to get on with things, and they never leave your side.

'Hello,' I say to the three blonde ladies waiting by the cricket club. I haven't seen them for a while; it's lovely to bump into them.

I immediately drop down and start stroking their dogs (that sounds like a rude euphemism, but it's not! I mean it literally).

They respond in kind. 'Hello, lovely Elvis,' they say, and my puppy replies by nuzzling up to them. In my pre-Elvis life, I'm sure they would have chatted to Juan about his outfit and ignored me. But not now - they want to know how he is and what we've been up to.

'My daily walks with Elvis have been a real revelation,' I say to Juan as we wave goodbye to them and walk on. Elvis skips up to a dog about four times his size and starts sniffing its bottom. 'I've learned so much about the area and understand the locale much better than before he came along.'

'Really? You mean - you have to walk around muddy parks all day now, but you didn't have to before.'

He's right, but there's something about the daily walk: an activity which you'd imagine would be rather mundane and performed out of duty rather than enjoyment is rendered whimsical and wonderful, thanks to a dog. Something about the unglamorous, humble, welly boots-beauty of it all brings you alive. The walks in all weathers, the sniffing, stopping, territory marking - it's all so real. The cold, frosty mornings, tired legs, sore feet, joy of it all.

I don't share this with Juan, of course. He's slipped his gilet on, adjusted his beret on his head, and walks beside me with his hands in his pockets. He looks bored. And I get that. I would have looked bored, too, until I got Elvis.

'Shall I give you a rundown of all the people I've met in the park?'

'Oh, go on then. Anyone famous?'

'No, of course not. But - do you see that guy sitting on the bench?'

I point over at the bench and watch Juan's surprise as he sees the old man sitting on the end of it with a scraggy old dog at his feet.

'He's here every day. He sits there, and whenever he sees me, he calls me Lady Mary; I don't know why. I call him Shaky because he's always misquoting William Shakespeare.'

'How would you know whether he was misquoting? Are you a Shakespeare expert all of a sudden?'

'You wait,' I say as we wander over to him.

'Good morning, Lady Mary. How are you on this fine day?'

'I'm very well, thank you. This is my friend Juan.'

'What a colourful get-up,' he says, surveying Juan's outfit. 'You two look like Romero and Julie.'

'Romeo and Juliet?' says Juan.

'The very same,' he says with a captivating smile.

I've never actually seen Shaky walking his dog. Instead, he seems to sit on the bench all day looking pensive and slightly apprehensive, waiting for someone, anyone, to come along and talk to him.

He doesn't seem unhappy, but at the same time, he seems to radiate sadness. I should probably spend more time getting to know him to see what the aura of sadness is all about. But maybe not now, with Juan hopping from one foot to the other and telling me how worried he is about ruining his favourite shoes.

'I'm going to head off,' he says. 'I'm just not cut out for this dog nonsense.'

'OK, lovely, I Completely understand; see you soon.'

CHAPTER 8

*I*t's early November, and the park is a different place now. Far fewer people are here, and the weather has turned. It's become bitterly cold first thing in the morning. I've bought Elvis a coat to keep him warm. OK, I'll be honest, I've bought him two coats and three jumpers, and I imagine I'll buy many more. And I have no idea whether he's cold, but he looks gorgeous in them all. Dressing him is so much easier and less fraught than dressing me. Gone is the worry about the judgement of the sales assistant as I flick through the racks, looking for a size 18. All I worry about with Elvis is picking something that keeps him warm and makes me smile.

'EXCUSE ME, EXCUSE ME,' shouts a man running across the park, holding something out in front of him. He's a very tall man who does not wear his height well...he's lean and angular, and his running action resembles nothing so much as a baby giraffe trying to put on a pair of trousers. He's all elbows and knees up by his waist. His glasses are askew on his nose.

I realise he's holding a phone out in front of him.

'It's Charlie,' he says.

I look more closely and realise that it's my phone that he's holding.

I look at him. What's going on?

'It's Charlie,' he repeats.

I take the phone from him and say 'hello,' cautiously, hating how his fingers brush mine as he hands it over.

'What's going on?' asks Charlie. 'I call you up, and some random guy answers and when I ask if you're there, he tells me he doesn't know, he's never heard of you, and he asks me to describe you.'

'I'm in the park,' I say. 'I don't understand what's going on.'

The skinny guy is standing there, staring at me.

'How did you have my phone?' I ask.

'I found it...over there, by the trees. I didn't know whose it was, so I was going to take it to the police station. Then it rang, so I answered it.'

'Oh, I see. I must have dropped it. Thank you so much.'

There is a puppy by the man's feet who looks very much like Elvis (obviously not as pretty). But, unlike Elvis, who is running around me, eager for me to throw the ball, this little one is lying on the ground, completely conked out.

'Is your dog OK?'

'She does that all the time; just ignore her,' he says.

The puppy doesn't move, and the man doesn't move. I don't particularly want to chat with Charlie in front of him.

'OK, well - thanks again for bringing the phone back.'

I walk off, throwing the ball for Elvis as I go, but when I look back, he's still standing there, staring after me, while the puppy lies at his enormous feet.

'Sorry, Charlie, this is all so weird.'

'Yeah - just a bit. I was only calling to see whether you and Elvis wanted to go to Joy's for a little tea party on Saturday. She's invited a few of the puppies and their owners, so you'll get to meet Elvis' siblings. And his mum.'

'Yes, of course, that sounds fun.'

'Fab will text you the details. Talk to you later. Make sure you keep hold of your phone.'

Looking back, I see the tall man standing there, watching me. He did me a great favour by returning my phone, but why the need to be so creepy?

I'm so busy looking behind at the man and his collapsed dog and wondering why he's lingering that I turn around and walk straight into someone.

'Oh, gosh - sorry - I didn't see you there,' I say. 'Are you OK?'

'I'm fine. Perhaps my coat isn't bright enough for you?'

The lady is wearing a beautiful, bright red anorak.

'Well, yeah, you'd think I would see you. It's a fab coat, by the way.'

While we exchange pleasantries, Elvis busies himself with getting to know the puppy in front of him.

Now, dogs are very different to humans in many ways. They walk on four legs, have fur all over them, and can't talk. That's just for starters. But in no way are they more different from humans than in how they greet one another. Elvis saunters round to the back of the puppy in front of him and shoves his nose into the other dog's bottom. The other dog is forced to tolerate the intrusion. Then they change places, and Elvis is sniffed.

Whatever this sniffing routine leads them to understand about one another seems to satisfy them both. So they run around the park together, skipping around one another, jumping up onto one another and generally wrestling as they play.

The dogs look very similar: Elvis is more shaggy-haired, while the puppy he's playing with is tightly curled, but they are the same size and colour, making it difficult to see when one dog ends and the next starts as they gambol together.

'Is that your puppy?' I ask the lady in the red jacket.

'Yes, that's Freddie. He's a cavapoo.'

'Oh wow - so is mine. He's called Elvis. They seem to like one another.'

She smiles at this. 'I'm Maria,' she says.

'Nice to meet you. I'm Mary. Mary Brown.'

CHAPTER 9

'met this really lovely woman in the park yesterday,' I tell Ted. 'She has a cavapoo called Freddie. She's in the police but isn't on the beat anymore, not since she had children. She does something in community policing or something. She's nice.'

'What? You just met her in the park?'

'Yes. Her name's Maria. I bumped into her because I wasn't looking where I was going.'

'You bumped into her, and somehow you exchanged names and the names of your dogs, and she told you all about her job, and you became friends?'

'Yes - we walked along for a bit, then decided to get a coffee. I'm meeting her again later.'

'How on earth do women do that? Just make friends. If I asked a random bloke in the park if he wanted to join me for coffee, he'd punch me in the face.'

'Have you ever tried befriending anyone in the park?'

'No, of course not.'

'Well then, you don't know what would happen - perhaps you'd make a new friend.'

'Yeah - I have enough mates; I'm not going to go trawling through the park to find some more.'

'Your choice,' I say. 'I have a lovely new friend, and I'm meeting her in half an hour.'

Ted shakes his head and grabs his tie, winding it around his neck and tying it in a big knot. Ties are the oddest pieces of clothing, aren't they? Men talk about the absurdity of women's fashion - but look at them all - tying a bit of material around their neck in the most uncomfortable way possible and leaving it there all day.

High-heeled shoes, pencil skirts, and peplum-waisted tops may seem odd, but there's a reason for them - to make women look taller and slimmer. So what's the justification for strangling yourself? Honestly - men are such funny little things.

I MEET Maria next to the boat club. From there, we walk past the cricket club and hear a rapping on the window and shouts from inside the club. Three blonde heads appear. The three beautiful blonde women wave at us and hold their puppies up.

I wave back furiously, as does Maria.

'They are really friendly. I was a bit nervous about them at first, given how glamorous they are, but I like them now. I sometimes see them waiting by the entrance to the cricket club. I don't know why they gather there...it's like they're waiting for someone.'

'Yes, they are,' says Maria. 'Did you not hear what happened?'

'No, I don't know anything about them except that they say hi when I see them in the mornings.'

'Oh gosh - well, they're sisters. And there were four of them, but Lisa died of cancer. It was awful.'

'Oh God, no. I had no idea.'

'Lisa was really beautiful. I know those three look great, but she was a stunner. It was so bloody sad.'

'How long ago did she die?'

'Oh, not long - maybe a year. A year at the most. She's buried at the churchyard over there.'

Maria points at the church nearby as she carries on talking. ' You know you said you see them waiting by the entrance to the cricket club? Well, they wait there for a reason. Lisa was always late; every time they met, she'd be the last to turn up, and they used to moan about having to wait for her. At the funeral, Sarah - the older sister - said how late Lisa always was, but how she would give anything to have to wait for her now. It was a really sad moment. So the three of them meet at the entrance to the cricket club to walk their dogs every morning, then wait for a while as if they're waiting for Lisa.'

'Ohhhh, is that what they're doing? I've seen them standing there in the past, but I had no idea why or what they were waiting for.'

'Yes - waiting for Lisa. Sorry, that's a depressing start to our walk,' she says. 'I didn't mean to be so maudlin.'

'Oh, that's OK,' I say. 'It's a very sad story.'

'Come on then, who else do you know in this park?'

I look up and see Roger and Pam in the distance. They are a couple whose names I know. I'm not sure why. With most people around here, I only know their dogs' names, but these two talk in such loud voices to one another that you can't help but hear their names.

'Roger, are you going to put him on the lead now?'

'No, Pam. I'm leaving him off today.'

All yelled as if they were 100 metres apart instead of standing right next to one another.

The two of them are always together. Pam is absolutely

lovely - she must be around 70, but she always has immaculate hair and a full face of makeup. And she dresses so nicely. I hope I'm as elegant as she is when I'm her age.

This morning she's in a cream and lilac V-neck top, a lilac silk scarf around her neck and a big cream coat. The sort of coat that would be filthy in about five seconds if I went for a dog walk in it. She waves at me as we approach while Roger stares off into space.

I'll be straight with you here - Roger is a bit of a dick.

'Morning,' I say. I've just thrown the ball for Elvis to chase, and he leaps into the air to retrieve it like a wild salmon jumping up out of the water. He brings it back and drops it right next to my foot while Maria's dog, Freddie, runs around him.

'Where does he get the energy?' asks Pam. 'Look at him. Little Disney dog - always dashing around.'

She always calls him Disney dog because she says his floppy ears make him look like 'Lady' out of Lady & the Tramp.

'I know, he doesn't stop,' I say.

'He runs too much,' says Roger, with unnecessary bluntness.

The two of them make the oddest couple - she's bright, warm, and chatty. He's a miserable oaf, but they seem to delight in one another's company and walk together daily. When I first saw them, I assumed they were married, but Pam told me they weren't.

She said: 'sadly not', which I thought rather strange. I'm sure that if Pam ever wanted to get married, she could find someone much more lovely than the rather miserable Roger.

'This is Maria,' I say, introducing my new friend.

. . .

WHILE MARIA and Pam smile at one another, I throw the ball up into the air, watching as it lands with a bounce. Elvis darts towards it. But then a familiar-looking dog scoops in and grabs it before he can get it. Oh God, not again.

Elvis looks at me as if to suggest that this is most irregular. The interloper has the ball fixed in its mouth and runs off at top speed. Elvis follows in hot pursuit, trying to catch the little scoundrel.

'Walnut, Walnut...' A cry comes from across the park as a dishevelled and irate woman lumbers towards her dog, waving at him with a bright blue ball thrower and urging him to give Elvis his ball back.

Oh, God. It's bloody Walnut again.

'It's not your ball, Walnut,' she says, approaching the little dog who appears to be loving every minute of the chaos he's caused. He has his owner, me, and Elvis running after him as he gallops away, ball in mouth, tail standing high.

'A treat, look. Treat,' says Walnut's owner holding out a hand laden with cheese.

Walnut's nose twitches appreciatively as he eyes the cheese, but the ball is still wedged between his teeth. We're both standing there, waiting to grab the ball the minute he lets it go. But Walnut is good at this. He's no fool. He drops the ball onto the grass but pushes it back under himself as he does so. He then grabs a handful of cheese before retrieving the ball before we can get to it and trots off at top speed with the heady mix of cheese and ball in his mouth. Elvis looks up at me and barks. He wants me to throw the ball. But I have no ball to throw.

Walnut's owner is becoming increasingly distressed as she runs off after her ball-carrying dog. He thinks it's a game. People are chasing him and giving him cheese; it's the greatest game in the world.

Walnut runs around the field for 15 minutes with us all in

pursuit. Elvis runs alongside us as we chase. From time to time, he looks at me with curiosity, wondering why we're all running around after this dog and why I'm not throwing the ball for him.

'In a minute, sweetheart,' I say. 'We need to get the ball back first.'

'That dog will get you fit,' says Maria, joining in the chase.

'Yeah, or kill me,' I say, panting furiously to try and get my breath back.

'Stupid dog,' says Roger, walking away.

Then, suddenly and unexpectedly, Walnut drops the ball and walks away. Elvis picks it up and trots off. All's right with the world.

'I need to sit down,' I say. 'I might have to push Shaky along the bench and perch on the end. I'm bloody exhausted.'

'Yeah, no problem, come on, let's head for the bench.'

I manage to get my breath back as we walk along, and by the time I plonk myself next to Shaky, I can breathe without gasping.

'To be or not to say…' he starts, but I interject before he can torture any more of the world's greatest prose.

'I've been running around after a dog who wouldn't give the ball back,' I say. 'I'm about to die.'

'Walnut, by any chance?'

'Yes. The very same. How did you know it would be him?'

'He's the greatest thief since Jesse James,' he giggles. 'His ability to steal balls is legendary around these parts.'

'It's a well-earned reputation that he has. Do you know that he even managed to steal the cheese that was being offered to get the ball back, and he still managed to keep hold of the ball at the same time as eating it? The ball stinks of cheddar now.'

Shaky laughs. 'You see all sorts down here,' he says. 'Oh God…'

'What's the matter?'

'Nothing...just someone I don't want to see. I'll be off. You take care. Watch out for Walnut! See you soon, Lady Mary.'

He stands up slowly, and I reach down to stroke Burns as the old dog lumbers to his feet. I stroke Elvis, too; he's sitting patiently at my feet, staring at the ball.

'Was it something I said?' says Maria, sitting beside me. 'You took one look at me and stood up to go.'

'Ha, not at all, my dear, not at all. Just someone out there who I'm not fond of.'

'If it's Roger you're looking at, I'm with you,' I say. 'I'm not a big fan.'

'Oh, me neither. He's a down-and-out rascal. I don't like him one bit.'

'The trouble is that I like Pam and those two are inseparable,' I continue. 'If you want to be friends with Pam, you're forced to talk to old misery guts as well.'

Shaky doesn't reply to this, so I keep going.

'I think those two are secretly in love,' I say.

'They seem to spend a lot of time together,' confirms Maria.

'Yes, and when I asked whether they were a couple, I'm sure she said they weren't, but she wished they were.'

'Really?' says Shaky. 'Did she say that?'

'I've seen how she looks at him, definitely in love,' says Maria. 'Though God knows why. She's much too good for him.'

'See you soon,' says Shaky. His head is down, and he walks slowly away.

CHAPTER 10

*T*his afternoon, Elvis has a pre-Christmas tea party to attend; I'm thrilled to say he's invited me as his plus one.

'This is grossly unfair,' says Ted as he watches me getting ready. 'I'm supposed to be the one who goes out to parties with you. Now it's all about Elvis. You love him more than you love me.'

Ted's only joking, of course (I think), but I've noticed him getting quite irritated by the amount of time and attention I bestow on my furry friend. Of course, I don't help the situation by talking to Elvis all the time as if he's a toddler.

'You talk to that thing more than you talk to me,' Ted complains. He also says: 'You're happy to tickle and stroke that puppy all night - where's my affection?'

It's just that Elvis is so much prettier than Ted and so pleased to see me all the time...and he doesn't bug me for sex (I'll be honest - my sex life has taken a real blow since Elvis started sleeping in the bed. I don't want to frighten him).

'Come on then,' says Mr Curmudgeonly. 'I'll give you a lift.'

I'm going for afternoon tea at Joy's house; she's the lady who sold me the puppy. There's also going to be a guy there who took one of the other puppies in the litter, and apparently, he is disturbed by the fact that the puppy keeps 'playing dead' all the time. He's rushed the little thing to the vet a dozen times, and there's nothing wrong with it. Joy thinks it might be reassuring if he met Elvis and me. I'm not sure how that will be reassuring, but it's a little afternoon off, and Charlie and Juan will be there, so it should be fun.

I wonder whether it will be freaky for Elvis to see his mum and one of his siblings again. Will he recognise them? Perhaps he'll rush to his mother and want nothing to do with me again.

'Right, here we go. I'll pick you up around 7 pm, OK?'

'Thanks, lovely,' I say to Ted, opening the car door and trying to control Elvis as he darts for the pavement, leaving me floundering for the lead. 'See you later.'

It's odd walking back into Joy's house. The last time I came in, I was rendered speechless by love for the little puppy who is now by my side. The gate barring the door has gone, as have all the puppies who greeted us last time. So now it's just the mother dog, Flossie, sitting in splendid isolation on a rather comfortable-looking dog bed. Elvis pays her no attention at all.

'Oh, my goodness, let's have a look at him,' says Joy, peering at my boy. 'Oh, he's handsome. He's the best-looking of all of them, you know.'

'And so well-behaved.' I say.

'I'm very glad. Do you want to bring him over to meet his mother?'

'No, I think he's fine here. I'm his mother now.'

As I say this, I realise how weird it sounds. How weird it is. How weird I am. I didn't used to be mad like this.

There's a loud knock on the door and the sound of

familiar voices, and I'm remarkably pleased that Juan and Charlie have arrived to save me from myself. They come rushing in and fuss over Elvis, admiring his new blue coat and stroking him relentlessly.

'Right, come on, let's have something to eat,' says Joy, walking into the kitchen. I take my seat at the table, but Joy walks out clutching two food bowls for the dogs.

'Oh, not us?'

'No, Robert will be here in a minute. Once he's arrived, we can eat.'

In the kitchen, I can see a couple of those lovely three-tier cake stands with piles of sandwiches on one layer, scones with jam and cream on the other layer, and cakes on the final plate.

My God, the food looks so delicious. I hope bloody Robert turns up soon, or I'll have to sneak in there and grab something when no one's looking.

'How's it all been going?' asks Joy. 'Elvis is looking very well.'

'It's been great. I love him so much,' I say. 'He makes everything so wonderful.'

'And was Ted OK with it all in the end? He seemed shocked when he answered the door and saw us standing there with a puppy.'

'Yes, to be fair to him, he came round to the idea remarkably quickly. He's been great.'

The arrival of Robert disrupts our conversation, thankfully, so I don't have to go into any more detail about the fact that Ted had no idea I had bought a puppy until Joy, and her daughter arrived on my doorstep carrying one.

The man who walks into the room is familiar, but I can't remember where on earth I know him from. He looks like Stephen Merchant, the 15' tall comedy actor.

'I know you!' he says. By his feet is a puppy who looks exactly like Elvis (but not as pretty).

'Do you? I think I recognise you, but I'm not sure where from.'

'It's Robert,' he says. 'Robert from the park. Do you remember? I found your phone when your friend was calling you. This is Astro, my cavapoo.'

'Yes, of course. Charlie rang, and you asked her to describe me. That's Charlie over there.'

'That was an odd moment,' says Charlie, explaining the story to everyone.

Then there's a small thud, and Astro falls over again and lies on her back by Rob's feet.

'Goodness, she's playing dead again. Does your puppy do that?' he says to me.

'No, definitely not. I've never even heard of a puppy doing that before.'

'This little one does it all the time. Scared me half to death at the beginning, but I've got used to it now. She's such a maniac.'

I remember him more clearly now - the way he came loping across the park, clutching my phone and handing it to me, his unfathomably-long fingers stroking mine as he passed it to me. The leering, uncomfortable weirdness of the man. I also remember that puppy lying on her back by his feet.

'Have you spoken to the vet?' I ask.

'Yes, many times. Not recently. But I went when she was younger and was reassured that she's healthy and well.'

'Maybe you need a dog behaviourist expert? Or have you tried googling? There might be a name for the condition?'

I feel forced into offering help and advice because of his proximity to me...leering down at me from a great height.

'Shall we sit?' he says to his puppy, who's still playing dead on the floor and taking no notice of him. Then he perches on the small sofa next to me while Elvis looks at Astro and begins swiping at the poor, prone creature with his paw in an effort to rouse him.

'I've tried googling the condition, look...' he says, pulling out his phone to show me what it says on Google.

But when he opens his phone, the image that greets me is way more shocking than some random, veterinary suggestions. It's a picture of me.

Yes - me.

My face beams out, and I look like a lunatic, clothed in the unflattering polystyrene green uniform they make us wear at work. He's obviously been looking at pictures of me on my work's website.

'Oh,' he says, closing the phone. 'Google probably hasn't got much to offer in any case.'

With that, he stands up and walks out of the room.

I look over at Charlie and Juan, but they are deep in conversation with Joy; neither notices the spectacularly embarrassing moment. I'm on my own here. Even Astro seems oblivious.

Robert is gone for 15 minutes, during which time I'm forced to play with a rather worried-looking Astro. The whole thing means that our food is further delayed. My insides feel like they are going to eat themselves. I'm in this hellish scenario where I can see the food piled up in the kitchen but can't eat it.

'We'll all have a good appetite by the time the food comes out,' says Joy.

I'll be dead by the time the food comes, I think. And real dead - not like this daft puppy that keeps collapsing at everyone's feet.

CHAPTER 11

*E*ventually, we do eat, and it is delicious. I try to exert some self-control, but fail miserably, and grab sandwiches and cakes as I've never grabbed food before in my life (this is probably not true...I'm a bit of a food grabber, generally speaking). I can feel Rob staring at me all the time, which is slightly disconcerting but certainly doesn't put me off consuming around twice as much as the others.

'Have you got to know many of the guys in the park?' he asks. 'There are some really friendly people there.'

'Yes, I know Roger and Pam, who take their dogs for a walk every morning.'

'Gladstone and Gwen.' he says.

'No, I think they are called Pam and Roger.'

'Yes, the people are called Pam and Roger. The dogs are Gladstone and Gwen.' 'Oh, I see. I thought I'd been calling them the wrong names all this time. They're really sweet. I think they may quite fancy one another. I was talking about it to the guy who sits on the bench. I know him as well. I like him.'

'That was you?'

'That was me, what?'

'Talking to Doug about Pam and Roger.'

'Wait. What? Who is Doug?'

'The guy who sits on the bench. You shouldn't have done that,' he says, shaking his head.

'Shouldn't have done what? What's the problem?'

'You shouldn't have told Doug that you thought Pam and Roger would get together. He's heartbroken. Devastated.'

'Is he? I'm really confused.'

'Yes. Pam and Doug were trying to get back together.'

'What?'

'They are married but recently separated. He is very keen to get back with her.'

'With Pam?'

'Yes - with Pam.'

'Oh, right. I didn't know any of this.'

'No, well, he doesn't talk about it much. But he sits on that bench all day, hoping to bump into her. I saw him this morning near Hampton Court bridge. He said he couldn't bear to go to the park in case he bumped into Roger and Pam because someone he likes very much, and trusts, told him that the two of them fancy each other. He's heartbroken. Does she even like Roger? I thought they were just friends.'

'Well, I thought she liked him. I'm confused.'

'Doug and Pam have been married for 40 years. He's desperate to get her back.'

'Oh no. I didn't realise any of this. I know Doug. I see him every day. I didn't know his name, though. I nicknamed him 'Shaky' because he's always quoting Shakespeare to everyone who walks past.'

Robert laughs at this. 'Yes, he's very funny. He thinks of himself as a literary genius but always talks nonsense.

'I feel really bad now.'

'We were all hoping that Pam and Doug would get back

together. Doug certainly was, and little Burns as well, I imagine.'

'Oh God, don't make me feel worse than I already do. I didn't know she'd recently split up from someone.'

'Well, yes.'

As we're chatting, I notice Astro has collapsed on the ground again, and Elvis is pushing the little dog's chest with his two front paws as if he's giving life-saving CPR.

In my bag, I hear my phone ringing. It's only 10 minutes before Ted's due to collect me. Hopefully, that's him saying he's outside, waiting for me. I want to go home now. I feel like I've caused all this upset. Ted will know what to do. But when I look at my phone, I see it's a withheld number.

'Hi, Mary, is that you?'

'Yes, who's this?'

'It's Maria...from the park. Freddy's mum. Sorry - I'm not on my phone; I'm on my son's phone. I just wanted to talk to you. I bumped into Shaky, although I now discover that he's called Doug, and you won't believe what he told me....'

'Did he tell you that he's married to Pam, and they recently split up, and he's desperate to get back with her, but I told him that she's about to date Roger.'

There's silence on the phone.

'I'm at afternoon tea, and one of the guys here told me.'

'Do you think we ought to go and do an intervention and tell Pam how much Doug loves her and wants her back?'

'Er...yes, OK. Where are you now?'

'Near Hampton Court Bridge with Doug. He was sitting alone by the river, looking very pensive. He just said, 'My love has flown away.' I'm going to take him to the Prince of Wales and buy him a drink. I wondered whether you wanted to come, and we could call Pam and invite her down.'

'I'll meet you there. I'm just waiting for Ted to come and

pick me up. I'll text you when I leave here. I'll have Elvis with me.'

'Yep - I've got Freddy with me, and Doug has Burns with him.'

'OK, it's a real puppy party. See you there.'

I put the phone away and look up at the faces staring at me, eager for an explanation. It's very tempting to carry on talking and not give them one, but they all look so intrigued that it would be cruel to leave them in the dark.

'That was my friend Maria, who I met randomly in the park. She is with Doug, who is declaring his everlasting love for Pam,' I explain. 'She's going to take Doug to the Prince of Wales, and I'll join her when Ted gets here. We'll talk to him and possibly call Pam and tell her that her husband wants her back.'

'Oh, wonderful. Wonderful. It's a Christmas miracle. I'll come, too,' says Robert.

'And us,' says Charlie, nudging Juan. 'I'll take my car and meet you there.'

'Yes, I'll come with you, doll,' says Juan.

There's a sharp knock at the door, indicating Ted's arrival.

I look back at Joy, sitting there, all confused, as her lovely tea party comes to an abrupt ending for reasons she doesn't understand.

'You're more than welcome to come, too,' I offer. `You can have a drink in the pub and meet all the nutters from the park.'

'Oh, yes, please,' says Joy, delighted to be asked to accompany us on this unlikely adventure.

So, when poor Ted rings the doorbell, he's greeted by quite a scene. First, there's Joy, whom he last saw when she arrived at our house, clutching a small puppy he didn't want. Then there's the tallest man in the world with an unfortunate manner and a clumsy gait. Then there's me. Oh, and three dogs.

'Sorry to be a pain, but we're on a sort of mercy mission,' I say. 'We need to go to the Prince of Wales because two old people are in love, but I made a mistake and said to one that another one liked someone else, but I don't know whether that's....'

'Stop,' says Ted. 'You lost me right at the start of that. Come on; I'll take you to the Prince of Wales.'

'Great.' I follow Ted out of the house, leading Elvis, and Rob follows behind, leading Astro. Following behind is Joy with Flossie.

'You're not all coming?'

'Yes, is that OK?'

'I don't know whether we'll fit everyone in. That's a lot of canine content you've got there.'

CHAPTER 12

*H*ere we are then. All in the pub, sitting in a big circle, with the dogs in the middle. Burns is fast asleep, Astro is playing dead (I really think that Rob should talk to some sort of pet psychologist about that damned puppy - it's not right the way he collapses all the time), while Elvis and Freddie run around them both, chasing one another in circles.

'I'm so sorry about what I said. I was just chatting; I didn't realise the significance of the words. I didn't want to hurt you in any way.'

'Oh, my dear, don't be silly. I don't blame you in the least. It's all my own stupid fault.'

'How do you mean?' asks Maria.

'Well, for not telling Pam how I feel. For not letting her know how much I love her. I've been sitting there every day just to catch a glimpse of her, and she's always with that rascal Roger. I'd thump him if I were a few years younger.'

'I think she just likes having company,' says Maria. 'There's nothing in it, I'm sure.'

'Nothing at all.' I say. Doug nods but doesn't seem convinced.

'How about if we phone her and invite her down here?' I suggest. 'We can say we're having a little gathering of all the people who meet in the park to walk their dogs. it's almost Christmas, that would make sense, wouldn't it?'

'Oh goodness, no. Let's not play any more games. I'm going to ring her and tell her that I want her back. Can I borrow someone's phone?'

I put my password into my phone and hand it to Doug and he pulls his glasses down over his nose and peers at it.

'How do I call?'

'Why don't you tell me the number and I'll put it in and hand it to you?'

He reels off their home phone number which I dutifully enter into the keypad before giving the phone back to him.

Doug wanders out of the pub, presumably in search of peace and quiet, away from the Christmas songs blaring out in the pub, and a little privacy in which to make the call.

He seems to have been gone for a long time, then - just when I think he's swiped my phone and run away with it - he reappears with a smile on his face.

'She told me to meet her, so I'm heading off,' he says. 'Come on Burns.'

He gives me the phone and holds my hand tightly during the exchange. 'Thanks, love,' he says. 'Thanks for making me call her.'

I GO HOME that evening and I dance with Elvis. We've been doing this since he was a puppy. I put on some music. 'I'm Happy' by Pharrell is a particular favourite. Then I start to dance, and Elvis goes up onto his hind legs and jigs next to me. I suppose it's not really dancing, in the common understanding of the word. It's more a case of moving randomly to music. But, then again, that's what dancing is, isn't it?

Elvis certainly seems happy, as we move on the spot, creating this bizarre tableau. Ted thinks we should apply to go on Strictly but I think we need to work on his foxtrot a bit first and his Viennese Waltz needs some refining. In any case, Elvis and I don't do it for fame or fortune. Our dancing is just an expression of love. Well, an expression of my love for Elvis, and a sign of his tolerance of me.

We don't jiggle around for long before Elvis starts jumping like he wants to be in my arms, so I sweep him up and hold him close to my chest while we move slowly. Pharrell is still belting out in the background, but I don't hear it. Elvis licks my face and we sway together. I can just about feel the gentle beat of his heart as he drops his head onto my shoulder and falls asleep.

If this isn't love, I don't know what is.

CHAPTER 13

'OK, I've sorted it,' says Ted. He looks extraordinarily pleased with himself.

'What have you sorted, my love? The Middle East crisis? The asylum seekers drowning out of sheer desperation to find a safe place to live?'

'Not quite. But I might have solved the problem of Elvis peeing on the floor because he can't get into the garden.'

This is glorious news to my ears. 'Go on...'

'I have ordered a dog flap to be fitted at the back, so he'll be able to go in and out as he needs to.'

'Really?'

'Yes, really.'

'And you don't think the landlord will mind?'

'I've checked, and he said that's fine. It will have to be in the wooden panel, and we'll have to repair it afterwards, but we're committed to this place for two years, so I think it's worth it.'

'That's wonderful,' I say.

'The only problem is that the guys are coming to fit it tomorrow, and I won't be around. I know you hate dealing with workmen, but if you want a dog flap fitted, you'll have to do it.'

Oh, God. I hate dealing with anything like this. All the questions that I don't know how to answer. I find it hell on earth.

Questions like: 'Madam, would you like a re-upholstered mint green diagonal screw leaf door or the regular burgundy mashed wood constituent, bald eagle screw laser door?'

I want to scream: 'I DON'T KNOW WHAT ANY OF THAT MEANS. I'm not sure I know the difference between a nail and a screw. So please do what you think is right, and don't ask me any more questions.'

Ted is looking at me as my mind races through all these awful questions they might ask.

'You'll be OK, won't you?'

'I don't know. Maybe we should wait until you're back.'

'No. You can handle this. They are coming tomorrow at 3 pm.'

'OK,' I say reluctantly.

So, the whole of the next day is ruined as I pace around the sitting room, dreading the arrival of the builders. I don't want to make loads of cups of tea, and I don't want to answer questions or deal with them in any way. I briefly consider creating a sign which says: 'I am deaf and dumb, pleased just install the dog flap and go home.' But I manage to stop myself, and at around 5 pm, there's a knock on the door, and two blokes stride into my house. I point them toward the dog flap and ask them if they want tea.

'No thanks,' says one.

'Just Earl Grey for me,' says another.

Blimey. Not what I was expecting. I make tea for the sophisticated builder and put it next to him.

'I don't know anything about building, and I doubt

whether I'll be able to answer any questions, but I'll be in the sitting room if you need me.'

'No problem,' says Earl Grey man, and I rush into the sitting room and curl up on the sofa. It's quite a cold day, even with the heating on, especially with the back door wide open. I saw Ted's sweatshirt lying on the side in the kitchen, so I go and get it and put it on, snuggling up into it. It needs a wash, and it's way too big, but that's the attraction of it.

'Hi, can we borrow you for a second,' says one of the builders. He looks shocked to see me all curled up on the sofa, half-climbed into the sweatshirt.

'Ahhh, I love this,' I say, indicating Ted's sweatshirt. 'It keeps me all cosy and warm.'

Once I'm outside, they explain that they can't fix the door because they have the wrong attachments with them, but it's all prepared and will only take a few minutes, so they'll come back tomorrow, and then it will all be good to go.

Elvis watches them as they clear up their stuff, fascinated by the sight of two unfamiliar humans in his house.

The next day, at 5 pm, the builders arrive to finish the job. I look quite a state when I answer the door because I'm still wearing Ted's sweatshirt.

I see them glance at me and look at one another. I feel the need to explain my rather odd appearance.

'Sorry, I slept in this thing last night. Just the size and smell of it. It was lovely to wrap myself up while my boyfriend's away.'

The look they give me indicates that I've given them far too much information, so I wander into the kitchen to put the kettle on.

As I get out a mug, I hear Ted opening the door.

'Hi lovely, you're home early,' I say.

He wraps his arms around me from behind.

'Have you missed me?' he asks, snuggling into the back of my neck.

'Of course I have.'

'And everything's been OK with the builders? No hellishly difficult questions?'

'Nope, not one. They're just outside finishing it off.'

'I'll take the tea out to them,' he says. 'Whose sweatshirt is that?'

'This? It's yours.'

'It's not mine,' says Ted. 'It says KDI Builders on the back...it must belong to one of the guys.'

'Noooooooooo.' I say. 'No. I wore it in bed last night, thinking it was yours.'

Not mine. Just take it off and put it over there, and they'll never notice you had it on.'

'They will. I told them that I slept in it last night. I tried to explain my scruffy appearance because I thought he was looking at me strangely.'

'Yeah, sweetheart...he was looking at you strangely because you're wearing his bloody clothes.'

'This is mortifying. I'll have to completely change my identity and move to the other side of the world.'

'Or you could explain, like an adult,' he says.

'This is not the time for adulting,' I say as I pull off the sweatshirt and hurl it onto the sofa, running into the bedroom and slamming the door behind me.

They leave half an hour later, accompanied by light-hearted banter and laughter. Ted appears at the bedroom door minutes later. 'I told them. They looked relieved,' he says. 'And they saw the funny side, so don't worry.'

CHAPTER 14

The next morning, I'm back in the park at my usual time. I have arranged to meet Maria at the cricket club to grab a coffee.

'You are the talk of the park,' she says as she rushes up to me, holding a cup of my favourite cappuccino.

'I'll be honest, Maria, to hear you say that is a dream come true. All I've ever wanted was to be talked about in this park.'

'Ha, ha. You must admit, though, that was an amazing thing we did...charging off to the pub with all our puppies and sorting out a marriage.'

'We must be nuts,' I say, laughing with her. 'Although if I kept my nose out of everyone else's business in the first place, it wouldn't have needed to be done in the first place. That taught me a very valuable lesson.'

'No, you always need to have your nose in everyone else's business, or life becomes incredibly dull. That's the most exciting thing to happen to me in years.'

We walk off into the park, sipping our coffees while the puppies dance around in front of us. Shaky and Pam (I'll never get used to calling him Doug) sit together on the bench, smiling into the middle distance as we approach.

'It's Cupid,' says Pam as she spots me.

'You mean - it's the raving lunatic,' I correct her. 'I'm sorry about what happened.'

'Don't be daft,' says Pam. 'It was my fault for joking with you that I wished Roger and I were together. I was only doing it to try and get Dougy to pay me more attention. I thought he was sitting on the bench every morning, chatting to everyone who passed to show me that he didn't need me anymore. Little did I know that he was sitting there to show that I already had his attention. Life can be very confusing at times, can't it?'

'Very confusing,' I agree. 'I'm glad you two lovebirds found your way back to one another.'

'Yes, she's the love of my life. I adore her.'

Then he turns to her and, predictably enough, he launches into a nonsensical Shakespear quote.

'Shall I compare thee to a summer's rose? Thou art Juliet, my own Juliet.'

Pam smiles indulgently.

'We'll leave you, young romantics, alone. Lovely to see you.' I say as we walk off towards the park's main section, throwing the ball with all our might and watching the puppies scamper after it as if their lives depended on it, leaping into the air to catch it and frolicking with one another to gain possession.

The ball entertains them for ages. I can never quite believe how much joy a dog can derive from chasing a ball. But then, I guess many humans are the same. You don't even have to throw it to engage Ted; the sight of someone kicking a ball on TV renders him helpless for around 90 minutes and compels him to drink lots of beer and shout obscenities at the referee.

. . .

Maria throws the ball off towards the basketball court where a fitness class is taking place. The puppies race over and begin to play with a little white puppy there, but instead of racing straight back with the ball so I can throw it again, they stay there, running after the little puppy. We watch as the white puppy stops, and they start to sniff it in that rather unsophisticated way that dogs have. Then Freddie attempts to mount the little dog from behind while Elvis attempts to mount from the side (bless him, we haven't talked about the birds and the bees yet).

'Oh my lord, she's probably on heat,' shouts Maria, rushing towards the tumble of dogs on the ground. The white puppy's owner is on the phone and oblivious to the scene developing behind her.

'Excuse me,' says Maria, lifting Freddie off the white dog and tapping the lady on the shoulder. 'Is your dog on heat?'

I throw the ball to tempt Elvis away from the scene, but he doesn't move...he keeps following the white dog and attempting to mount her. I can see Freddie struggling desperately to get out of Maria's arms.

The phone lady finally ends her call and confirms that she thinks her puppy might be in heat. She picks her up, Freddie is returned to the ground, and the order is temporarily resumed.

But not for long.

I can see Freddie and Elvis looking around for the white puppy who smells so nice. When they spot her being carried, they leap up to try and reach her. Elvis is walking on his hind legs next to the lady, trying to stretch up and reach the dog, while Freddie is jumping up and down next to them like he's on a trampoline.

For reasons incredibly hard to understand, the lady then

puts the little white dog down, and the two male dogs leap on top of her. I look at Maria in horror as the two of them start licking her and growling to themselves.

It's all a bit too much for a park on a cold winter's day.

'I think you need to take her away,' I say as Maria and I both lean in to take our romantic puppies away. Remarkably, the two male puppies aren't fighting with one another at all. Instead, they are just sharing her.

The lady picks the white dog up and walks away. She doesn't communicate with us at all; she wanders off while our puppies follow behind.

And this is where the problems start because there is nothing we can do. I mean - nothing - to stop our boys from chasing behind her, jumping up at her, and trying to reach the female puppy. We both shout, throw the ball and run behind, clutching treats. I've never seen Elvis ignore a thrown ball before, and I've never seen Freddie ignore a treat. It's as if they are compelled by something greater than themselves.

Maria and I catch up with them, which isn't easy because the woman with the dog is moving at a considerable speed to get away from them. So, we're all running - three women and three dogs running through the park after one another like we're in some Benny Hill sketch.

Then she stops, and the puppies think that all their Christmases have arrived at once. So they jump up at the object of their affection.

'Can you take your puppies away,' cries the woman. 'Can't you see that I'm having trouble here?'

'Yes, that's why we've been chasing you to try and catch you so we can do that.'

I pick up Elvis, Maria grabs Freddie, and we turn and walk the other way. I don't know how Maria is coping, but I am having the mother of all struggles to keep Elvis from dashing straight back to the bitch on heat.

It's only when the woman is completely out of sight and the two of them have been handed many treats, and the ball, that they eventually calm down and start playing together again.

IN FRONT of us is the cluster of trees where the Scout groups and holidaying children make their camps in the summer. This morning, Elvis and Freddie go racing up to it and bark furiously at the trees and bushes. Finally, they venture into the den created by the foliage, then rush back out, making a lot of noise as if scared by something in there. Elvis has even dropped the ball and is ignoring it as he runs in and out of the trees.

'It's probably just kids misbehaving,' says Maria.

'Just ne'er-do-wells who are missing school to smoke in the bushes. I've never done anything like that,' I say.

'Me neither. Never. And I didn't crimp my hair during the German lesson because Vicky Johnson dared me.'

'You crimped your hair? What? You plugged in the crimpers in the class, waited for them to warm up, then went about the crimping process, all while you were learning how to say 'where's the station?' in German?'

'Yep. I'm hugely talented when it comes to multitasking.'

The puppies rush back into the trees, and we follow them to see what's happening. As we do, Elvis comes racing back out again.

Then I see why.

In the centre of all the trees and bushes stands a small man covered in tattoos and dressed in shorts and flip-flops despite the inclement weather. All of this is alarming enough, but nothing like that is alarming compared to what he is doing... walking a large goose on a lead.

Freddie races away from the scene, while Elvis runs back in and around the goose while the bird snarls and spits at him, forcing him to run back out again while Freddie runs back in. They are like some bizarre goose-chasing tag team.

'He's my pet. I'm not going to hurt him, says the man, adding: 'I have to walk him, or he won't be healthy.'

'Of course. No problem at all. Don't mind us. We just came in to see what our puppies were making such a fuss of,' I explain.

'I am Igor, and this is Boris, the goose,' he says.

'Nice to meet you. I'm Mary, and this is Maria. That puppy is Maria's, he's called Freddie, and mine is called Elvis. He's around here somewhere.'

'I live on that boat there,' he says, indicating one of the many houseboats lining the riverbank. The boats we always avoid walking past because the smell of drugs coming off them is enough to knock us out.

'I have heard of someone walking a pet goose in the park, but I always thought it was a bit of a myth,' says Maria.

'Nope - I'm real. Not a myth. And this is a pet. I'm not trying to feed him up for Christmas or anything like that. I love him and want to look after him.'

'Of course. He's a lovely pet,' I say.

'He's the best.'

Freddie runs around the man and his goose, but I can't see Elvis.

'Where's Elvis gone?' I say.

'Probably just preparing to rush back in again and run around the goose.'

But something doesn't feel right. Where is he?

I push my way out of the bushes and look around. There's

no sign of him. His ball is lying there...discarded on the ground. But where is my puppy?

'Elvis, Elvis,' I shout, running away from the goose and the oddly-dressed man. Suddenly they don't seem so amusing anymore.

Where is he?

'Elvis, Elvis.'

I start to walk around to try and catch sight of him. But, oh no, he hasn't run after the bloody dog on heat, has he?

I head in roughly the same direction she was heading when we last saw her. But there's no sign of her. I'm not sure where to go; there's no one around. It's so unusual; this park is usually packed.

I walk towards the little children's area in the park's centre. There are usually people there. Perhaps Elvis went there to play with the children. I can see people milling around outside the park. Great. Someone must have seen him. Elvis is such a gorgeous, friendly little thing; he must have gone up to one of them.

Then I see her - the woman walking the dog on heat.

Oh, thank God.

I race up to her, shouting for her to stop. She sees me coming and slows down.

'Have you seen Elvis?'

'I think he's dead, isn't he?'

'What?'

'He's dead. He died years ago.'

'No - Elvis, my puppy. The little one looks like a teddy bear. He was trying to get to your puppy. He's called Elvis. I can't find him anywhere. I thought he might have come looking for you.'

'No. Sorry.'

I can see her face soften now she realises that I'm a

woman who's distressed because she's lost her puppy, not a lunatic trying to find long-dead pop stars.

'How long ago did he run off?'

'About 10 minutes ago.'

'Oh damn, they can get quite a long way in 10 minutes.'

Yeah, not helping at all.

We're both scanning the horizon.

I don't want to stand here and do nothing, but I have no idea what to do. Everywhere I run might be taking me further away from him.

'I don't know what to do,' I say. 'He's so little, and he's all lost.'

'I'm sure he'll reappear,' she says. 'He's only been gone 10 minutes.'

'But you just said that….'

'Yep, I shouldn't have said that. Sorry.'

She puts her puppy down.

'Do you want me to come round with you to look for him?'

'I don't know.'

'Are you here on your own? What happened to your friend?'

'She's in the bushes with a tattooed bloke. She's looking at his goose. Not a euphemism.'

'It's probably better if we both look in different places,' I say. 'Can I give you my number in case you see him?'

I start walking to the river in case he's walked over there. Elvis hates water, so I don't think he'd jump into the river, but what if he slips? The rain's getting harder now, and my panic is rising. It's cold and wet, and I've no idea where he is.

I start running. I don't know where to or why I'm running - it just feels like I need to cover this park with some urgency. But I don't know where to go.

'Elvis, Elvis.'

I see a man with a sausage dog, exactly the sort of dog that Elvis likes to play with. I race over to him, waving my hands like a crazy woman.

'Stop, stop,' I shout.

'I can't find my dog, and I don't know which way he's gone or anything,' I shout. 'Have you seen him?'

I make a rather terrible attempt to describe him, but I'm crying so much I don't think I'm making a very good fist of it.

'Don't worry; he won't have gone far. I'll look out for him,' says the man. Everything's a blur. I don't know where to start looking. I don't know what to do. I feel desperate - angry with myself for turning my attention away from him and terrified that he might be out there, lost and looking for me.

More than anything, though, I'm just petrified that someone has taken him. I remember all the warning posters in the vets, and I've heard the stories...the posts on Facebook from people desperate to find their puppies and the realisation that they have been stolen.

It's starting to rain a lot now, and the park is huge. I don't know what to do. Finally, Maria comes running up behind me, and I burst into tears.

'I can't see him. I don't know where he is. I want my Elvis back. Please help me.'

CHAPTER 15

*I*t's 8 pm, and I'm bereft. I'm shattered. I've never felt like this in my life before. I know he's only a dog, and I'm being silly, but I don't know what I'll do if I can't find him. I don't know how I'll be able to go on. He's such a huge part of my life.

'Hey, come on...we're going to find him,' says Juan, hugging me closely while we stand in the park. Ted is in front of us with a stern look on his face. He rushed out of work when I called him to tell him what had happened and has been helping me comb through the park ever since. So now Charlie and Juan are here, and Joy, along with Robert, whose daft puppy, is playing dead the whole time. A couple of the guys from work have turned up, too. It's dark, so we all have our phone torches on. I'm desperate for us to have a good look everywhere before nighttime. I don't know what I'll do if we don't find him then. I've told Ted that I am sleeping in the park. And I was only half-joking when I said it.

'Juan - I don't know what I will do if we don't find him before bedtime. He can't stay out here all night on his own.

I'm not going home, knowing my little boy is out here looking for me.'

'I know, angel, I understand. Let's concentrate on finding him, shall we? Positive mindset. We can find him. There's a little group of us now. It's all going to be OK.'

As we talk, I see a trail of people approaching us. Maria leads them...there's Doug and Pam at the front, followed by Roger and three friends. There's the woman I met earlier with the bitch on heat, and then I see the group of lovely blonde women who wait by the cricket club every morning. I feel like crying with relief. Walnut and his owner have come to join in, along with a few other people, many of whom I recognise from seeing them in the park but haven't got to know.

'We're all here for you,' says Pam. 'Just tell us what you need us to do.'

I burst into tears again at this point. I throw myself into Pam's arms to thank her because I cannot speak through the sobs.

'Listen up, everyone,' says Ted. 'We've only got until 9 pm until the park closes, but by that time, given the incredible number of people who have come to join in the search, we should have scoured every inch of the park. Elvis isn't a very confident little thing, so he might have tucked himself away in the bushes. There's a chance that he's injured. We need to be sure that he's nowhere to be seen in the park. The next step - if you are all up for it - will be to go knocking on doors in the area. I've made some flyers that we can put through letterboxes.'

There are murmurs of agreement.

'I'm not sure how to divide everyone up,' says Ted. 'I don't know the park as well as those of you who walk here every day.'

'I know every inch of this pace,' says Robert, stepping

forward with his madly long legs. 'It's easily divided into five sections.'

He quickly counts the number of people and decides that there are 27 people.

'OK, could everyone except for Mary and Ted get into a group of five,' he instructs.

'Gosh, he's good at this,' I say to Ted.

'Not really,' he replies. 'Any fool could have worked it out.'

The groups are created and given their jurisdictions. For example, one group is over by the river, another is at the cricket club end, and another is at the playground end. The other two groups will check either side of the meadows.

'Ted and Mary, you should be free to roam and look wherever you think he's most likely to have gone. Does that sound OK?'

'Yes - thank you, you're a star.'

The groups are told to return at 8.45, and if they see anything, they should phone me. Then they all disappear, and I make my millionth silent prayer of the day that Elvis will be found safe and well.

I suppose my biggest worry is that Elvis has fallen into the river...that's the image that sneaks into my imagination whenever I think of him and where he might be, so I head over with the river group to help them.

Ted is coming with me. We hold hands as we walk along the river to the section nearest the trees where Elvis first went missing.

'Ah, there you are,' says a man in a large overcoat. 'I've been looking for you.'

It takes me a while to realise that this is the man we met earlier, walking his goose in shorts and flip-flops (him, not the goose). I feel unreasonably angry with him because it was when I was talking to him that Elvis disappeared. If he hadn't come along when he did, Elvis and I would be at home, curled up on the sofa by now. I walk away before I say something unfair to him.

Ted talks to him, though, and seems to persuade him to join the search because the next thing I know, he has a torch and a stick and is hunting through the undergrowth. But, to be fair to him, he's looking very carefully at everything, going through the leaves lying on the ground, moving branches, and climbing into the gnarled winter bushes in search of my puppy.

I decide to go over and thank him for coming to help us. The guy doesn't even know me; it's very kind of him to leave his goose behind and rummage through the undergrowth for me.

'What colour is the dog we are looking for?' he asks when I arrive by his side.

'He's a sort of teddy bear colour,' I say.

'So, a bit like your dog, then.'

'Well, yes – it's my dog we're looking for.'

'What?' he says, suddenly stopping his digging.

'Yes, it's Elvis. My dog. Do you remember you met him earlier today?'

'Yes, that's what I came off my boat to talk to you about, but the man over there told me not to speak to you because you were busy hunting for his lost dog. He asked me whether I would help him to find his dog.'

'Yes.'

'So, whose dog is missing?'

'My dog. Our dog. That man is my boyfriend; the dog belongs to us.'

'Oh, this is weird then because your dog is on my boat.'

'Oh my god, are you joking? Please tell me you're not joking?'

'I'm not joking,' he says. 'He's fast asleep with the goose.'

I burst into tears at this stage. Maybe the 900th bursting

into tears of the day. 'Please let me see him, please....' I say, grabbing the guy's arm and shaking it to illustrate my urgency.

'Come on then, come on to the boat,' he says. 'The dog was sitting by the boat when I got back earlier; when it started to rain, I brought him on board to keep him dry. He's fine. I came straight to find you, but you weren't there.'

I follow him to his boat and peer through the window to see Elvis; he's not curled up with the Goose. Instead, he's asleep on a small bed that's been fashioned out of blankets while the Goose lies next to him.

Igor opens the door, and I rush in and over to Elvis. When he sees me, he immediately jumps into my arms and falls back to sleep. The warmth of his body against my skin feels like it's bringing me back to life. I can feel the gentle beat of his heart, and I'm reminded of the many times we have danced together at night.

'Thank you,' I say to the man. His cabin is filthy, and it stinks to high heaven of cannabis. I don't know how that poor goose survives it. I step gently off the boat and walk over to Ted.

'Oh my God - Elvis,' says Ted, dropping the stick he was using and wrapping his arms around both of us. Elvis lifts his head and licks Ted's face before dropping his head down onto my shoulder.

'His fur smells of drugs,' says Ted. 'I mean, really smells of drugs. He's going to get us arrested.'

'I don't care,' I say. 'I don't care about anything except this little angel.'

CHAPTER 16

*I*t's Christmas Eve. It's also Elvis's first birthday. He's a year old. We have survived a year as dog owners. Now we're celebrating in style with a puppy party. We've invited everyone we've met over the last 12 months and their dogs. There are some old friends here, too, like Charlie and Juan standing right back against the wall, away from the marauding animals.

'There seem to be more puppies here than people,' I say. 'Have some puppies sneaked in without owners?'

As I look down at my notes, there's a murmur of laughter at this. I can't believe that I offered to give a speech. Who gives a speech at a puppy party? I must be stark, raving mad.

But I just wanted to tell everyone how fab he is; how fab all dogs are. I know it hasn't been easy, but it's all been worth it, and people need to know that. Every cleaned-up wee, every ball thrown, every walk in the cold is worth it. And look at him now on his first birthday - all grown up and dressed to kill in his reindeer outfit.

'Elvis is mad,' I say. 'Of course, he's mad. All dogs are mad. They're little, loveable lunatics - all of them.

'There are a few things that Elvis does that make me laugh...the way he growls like a gorilla when anyone knocks at the door but then hides behind the sofa when they come in.

'There's his obsession with brushes - floor brushes, shaving brushes, clothes brushes and nail brushes. He barks like crazy whenever he sees one. But he saves his real anger for hairbrushes. My goodness, he does not like them. He goes insane if I try to brush my hair, dragging the brush off me and running away with it, hiding it under the sofa where I can't find it. When we first had him, I remember going out without brushing my hair because he would go wild when I tried to brush it.

'And he doesn't like it when animals come on the television - he can't abide that. And he's paralysed by fear when he hears a bin lorry reversing. And he's not keen on balloons either...I mean, he's fine when they're not blown up, but if he sees you blowing them up, he barks and barks at them, then runs and hides.'

Elvis is curled up next to me on the sofa as I speak, looking at me with those eyes of melting chocolate, set in the face of furry beauty. The other puppies are playing on the floor, but he seems content to stay there, all curled up next to me.

'He is such a pretty little thing, but he doesn't always do very pretty things...in common with all dogs, he likes nothing more than sniffing a backside. He enjoys licking his genitals and savouring the joyous scent emanating from piss-stained bins and lampposts.'

People are laughing and nodding at this stage, so I know I've got the tone right.

'And his love of socks. He's absurdly drawn to them. Also, slippers, flip flops and ballet pumps. But mainly socks. He grabs a sock and trots off with his tail held high, giving off an air of triumph as he parades his little trophies.

'There's so much I could tell you about this little dog...how much I miss him when he's not here, and how much I love coming back home to see him standing there, thrilled at the sight of me.

'Puppies are the best. So let's hear it for the puppies.'

Everyone raises their glasses, and we drink to puppies.

'Let's get the music on,' I say.

Tunes belt out of the system, puppies roam the apartment and Christmas decorations twinkle under the fairy lights. Of course, I don't expect any of the decorations, or even the tree, to be standing at the end of the evening. Elvis has pulled the tree down so many times I don't know why we bother putting it upright again, but I know that none of that matters.

I've been very lucky in my life...I found love, real love, when I met Ted. Now I know a different love: the love that a loyal pet can give to an owner and how love can be reciprocated.

Merry Christmas, everyone, but especially to all you puppies out there: you're all mad, but we love you.

ALSO BY BERNICE BLOOM

MORE BOOKS TO READ:

There are lots of books starring Mary Brown. They are all available here:

UK:

https://www.amazon.co.uk/Bernice-Bloom/e/B01MPZ5SBA?ref=sr_ntt_srch_lnk_1&qid=1640013061&sr=1-1

US:

https://www.amazon.com/Bernice-Bloom/e/B01MPZ5SBA?ref=sr_ntt_srch_lnk_1&qid=1640013098&sr=8-1

If you have any questions, feel free to email me at: bernicenovelist@gmail.com

Printed in Great Britain
by Amazon

19410914R00061